POINT OF HONOR

POINT OF HONOR

DAVID GETHIN

Charles Scribner's Sons
New York

First published in the United States by Charles Scribner's Sons 1985

Copyright © David Gethin 1984

Library of Congress Cataloging in Publication Data

Gethin, David.
  Point of honor.

  Originally published as: Jack Lane's Browning. 1984.
  I. Title.
PR6057.E76J3   1985   823'.914   84-23642
ISBN 0-684-18291-2

1 3 5 7 9 11 13 15 17 19   H/C   20 18 16 14 12 10 8 6 4 2

Printed in the United States of America.

Chapter 1

THE SECOND MAN, hooded and desperate, was running towards me. I slammed my foot down on to the accelerator, hard. The B.M.W.'s forward surge thrust me backwards into the driver's seat. An instant later, even amid the smell of burning rubber, the chaos of wrecked vehicles and the crackle of sub-machine-gun fire, the impact as the car hit the target was suddenly sickening. Involuntarily, my left arm went up to protect myself. The dark human shape slammed against the windscreen, then bounced limply away. The glass patterned into a crazy, frosted, fragmented kaleidoscope. More rubber burned as I wound the steering wheel. The car slewed sideways, smashing against the warehouse wall. I was free from the wreckage quickly and crouched low, Magnum in hand. The cacophony of klaxons, the anti-terrorist police, disgorging from the skidding armoured vans like demented drones, disorientated me for one fatal split second. A third opponent appeared to my left. He was close enough for me to see the bright, evil eyes through his balaclava slits. As I lined the Magnum instinctively, his Skorpion was firing. A triple impact hit me. I was falling, it seemed endlessly, the blood soaking through my shirt, damp and glutinous. On my back now and I was paralysed. Except for my left leg which jerked spasmodically, uncontrollably. The base of my spine was saturated with my own blood. In the whirlpool of sensory death I was out of control, falling helplessly, spiralling downwards towards the ultimate oblivion. . . .

I sat upright, instantaneously awake. Perspiration had soaked the bedclothes and my left leg was numb. I had been sleeping on it again. Desperate for reassurance, I focused my eyes on my familiar suitcase in the corner of the room. Yes, it was my suitcase. Yes, I was sitting up in bed, alive. The horror of my death was just another nightmare. Then the telephone rang. I was firmly back in reality now . . . a ringing telephone.

"Didn't disturb you, did I?"

The voice belonged to Ames. My alarm clock showed 4.15 pm. What did Ames want now? I had been with him at 11.20 am, which was when he had told me to get some sleep.

"No," I replied. "I had to get up to answer the phone."

"Sir Simon Verity at the Home Office has something for you, a study of stress on operatives."

"He's picked the right man. I know all about stress, and lack of bloody sleep."

"He'll discuss the matter with you this evening, at a party he's giving. Where shall his car collect you?"

So, proper Home Office. A chauffeur-driven car. And something in Ames' voice told me he was not speaking from his own phone. That meant the usual pick-up point was out, its location being known only to Ames and myself. I yawned and my tired body ached. Who the hell was Sir Simon Verity to disturb my private nightmares?

"Outside the Gents on the Dilly. Make and reg of transport?"

Ames found my choice of location amusing. He was laughing inwardly. I scribbled the number and letters R.R. on the bedside pad under the name Karen. Now who was Karen?

"Nineteen hundred sharp, Halloran. Should give you time to pop down to Moss Bros and hire an evening suit," Ames chuckled.

I hung up on him. Not only was it a lousy joke but it meant that he wanted a private word before I met this Verity. And if Ames wanted a private word, it usually meant bad news. Like me sticking my neck out. And I was tired of sticking my neck out. I had done so in West Germany the previous night. The lack of sleep leading up to that fiasco had done little to improve my usually liverish disposition. And on top of all the pressure, I had experienced that bad dream, again.

I had opted for voluntary retirement at the end of the month. In West Germany that bad dream had almost come true. A trigger-happy neophyte from Border Nine had set up a cross-fire and got me caught in it. I had wanted the girl alive, and not only because I have a predilection for live girls. This little cracker was walking information on what her chums had done with the Ambassador. Thanks to Willy the Kid, the left-handed gun from Lüneburg, what was left of her looked like a test target from a machine-gun factory. So it took me three days longer than necessary to locate the poor diplomat. He was almost out of his mind, not to mention dehydrated through lack of his customary sherry. They had nailed him in a box with the minimal life-support systems and buried him in a graveyard. Not very original, but thoughtless, even for them. What really reduced the entire business to some kind of horrific farce was the two surviving hooligans squealing to any reporter innocent enough to listen that I had been deliberately shooting to kill.

It was the old story and I had promised myself the next time anyone used it on me I would quit. But that wasn't the only reason. After fifteen years in my kind of work, the odds on being around to collect your derisory pension got shorter every month. Besides, I had seen and done enough. Only that morning Ames had provisionally agreed to keep me off the streets for the next week. Then I could legitimately wave the old bastard "goodbye". Now he had let the aristocracy disturb my sleep.

The bathroom mirror reflected my thirty-eight-year-old face unsympathetically. I was looking old. I had started to lose my hair and the etched lines were not funny any more. I scowled back at the mirror and took a hot shower. The foil head on my electric razor shattered into tiny pieces as soon as I switched the damned thing on. Sod's Law — no spare. Eventually I located the reserve razor, and an hour later one clean-shaven Halloran was in the lounge bar of the Oak.

Ames was on time, moving silently through the early-evening stockbrokers and the office-bound who needed three large ones before facing the wife, kids and the home computer. He ordered beer which meant he had been lunching at someone's club and guzzling claret. Too much wine at midday always made Ames thirsty by opening time.

"Cheers!" He raised the straight glass and settled into the leather seating in the corner of the wood-panelled lounge. The Oak was Ames' kind of pub: brass carriage lamps and pewter-topped tables, discreet talk and malt whisky on the optics.

"You unscrambled my message so you must be awake."

He stretched his long legs and lit a cigarette. Ames was six foot two, whipcord lean and hard. The dark hair greying around the temples was cut neatly, short like you would expect an ex-S.A.S. Colonel to keep his hair. The dark, pinstripe suit, the highly polished shoes and the rolled umbrella were all part of the Whitehall uniform. He looked like a civil servant in the forty to fifty bracket. But the hardened hands and the cold grey eyes were the give-away. Ames inhabited the Hall of Mirrors, that nether region of Counter-Intelligence and Security where seven pairs of eyes were a prerequisite for existence. He also mingled with the conspirators at the source of real power, that cabal of cold men who took the decisions no-one would ever publicly admit were taken.

"What goes on in the Star Chamber?" I asked.

Ames smiled. He had known me a long time and was aware that I viewed the whole murky world through cynical eyes. Years ago he had given up trying to tell me half-truths. His answer would be reliable.

"I'm not really sure. Mowlam from the Cabinet Office rang just after you left this morning. I trundled round to Whites as instructed and was introduced to Sir Simon Verity who supposedly handles Security Administration at the Home Office. They plied me with whisky and Mowlam sloped off. Verity wined and lunched me and told me about his department carrying out a study of stress and working environment on Security operatives. Eventually he asked if he could have a man from Omega Section. Before I pleaded the usual excuse of overwork he mentioned you were retiring at the end of the month and would therefore do very nicely. Know him by any chance?"

"Never heard of him," I replied.

"A very diplomatic request. He apologized for rocking the boat by checking Omega Section Records without my direct authority."

"Creep. You don't buy that story, do you?"

"Difficult to judge. Although in my experience whenever a civil servant or a politico apologizes in advance they usually have an undeclared motive."

Not just a pretty face, Ames. No-one from Omega Section was ever deployed without his authority. He also initiated action off his own bat. Mowlam was the only man entitled to be curious about Omega Section. And they only let Mowlam do that because he was the supreme conspirator in what I called the Star Chamber. Or, to put it another way, God in an earthly manifestation. Mowlam ran the Joint Intelligence Committee and answered in person to Downing Street.

Ames was also a very powerful and well-connected face.

"A word to the wise, Halloran. Watch yourself on this one. You should be the first Omega man to achieve retirement after seven years in the field. So stay in one piece for the next fortnight."

Which was Ames' way of telling me the Star Chamber were at it again.

Chapter 2

SIX FIFTY-NINE PM January 24th. A cold Friday in Piccadilly Circus. Murchison of Vice was disguised as a pimp, watching the gay traffic and the porcelain pushers. Another practitioner of streetcraft, Murchison. We exchanged professional courtesies by ignoring each other.

The Rolls-Royce pulled up as instructed, much to Murchison's almost visible annoyance: probably a throwback to the days when policemen looked the part and did point duty. I opened the rear door myself as the chauffeur glanced back at me over a broad shoulder.

"Halloran," I announced, settling myself back on the comfortable upholstery. This was no Ministry car. Verity's very own conveyance; the personalized number plates had been the giveaway. I soon discovered another personal touch, twelve-year-old malt whisky.

"How soon do we arrive?" I asked.

"Forty minutes or so, depending on traffic." Then, as an afterthought: "Sir."

I cast an occasional glance behind us, to make sure no-one was following. Second nature in my line of work. The Havana Coronas were in a box next to the whisky. I could see the chauffeur glance sneakily into the mirror to see if I knew how to treat a good cigar. He seemed disappointed I did not bite the end off.

My retirement plans had probably gone out of the window. So I settled back and enjoyed the whisky and the Havana. Verity had robbed me of my sleep. The least I could do in return was liberate his malt. We drove through Wimbledon towards New Malden on the A3 and I lost interest in the route.

Ames was sceptical about the story. And Ames had been around. I had first met him in Belfast. At the time I was with Army Intelligence — undercover in all the Ulster glamour spots. Then my face got known on the streets, dirty hostile streets that gave the inhabitants no hope; their ghetto undercurrents finally surfaced. I transferred out of that business after four big Micks jumped me in the Falls Road and I had to shoot my way out. There was a fuss about that. Some lawyer wanted me prosecuted for shooting unarmed civilians. Sure, they were unarmed by the time the lads from the depot and the R.U.C. arrived. Because the scavenging neighbourhood harpies had come out on cue, hoping to gouge my eyes out. All they got were their menfolk's guns. Funny how no-one bothered to ask why there were two 9mm bullets in my left leg.

I should have seen the light then and quit the Security business altogether. Dirty, insoluble war, Ulster, where the lads in khaki are walking Aunt Sallys and the politicians are dull enough or maybe devious enough to pay the populace to carry it on. I had lost some good mates out there and I vowed never to go back. So I made the mistake of being talked into a new job by Ames.

The medics had taken the two 9mm balls out of my leg. One left me with a slight limp if I have to run. Ames kept bending my ear about joining an outfit he was putting together called the Omega Section. No Ulster involvement but the Hell's Angels of the Security world nonetheless. Eventually I agreed. Now, seven years later, I had been the top operative for five years. Ames and I worked well together, probably because our senses were honed Sheffield-bright in the business of staying in one piece: he in the mirrored halls of conspiracy, with me out on the streets.

The Rolls stopped in the grounds of a country house. The chauffeur opened the rear car door for me. I handed him the empty whisky glass. Teach you to look down your nose at the lower orders, chum! I found a way through the assorted mass of Aston Martins, Ferraris, Porsches, Bentleys and Rolls-Royces which indicated it was a party for only the best people. So what was I doing here? I expected a butler to answer the porticoed front door. I was not disappointed.

Inside was the kind of sophisticated bedlam possible at only the best society parties, or so I imagined. A tray of champagne glasses materialized before me, held by an almost unnoticeable waiter. Then the discreet effect was spoiled by a bunch of chinless wonders and their hangers-on who assaulted me with a silly party hat.

"Conga time," they chorused.

"I'm with the caterers," I replied, sidestepping the lurch. No way was I there to provide the cabaret.

My assailants spotted another unsuspecting soul and latched on to him instead. The meandering mess wound its way through the hallway and out into the grounds. It was cold outside. I hoped they would die of exposure or drown in the ancestral lake. The butler obviously hoped likewise. He closed the door after them.

I felt a light touch on my arm and turned to see five-four of ash blonde smiling hospitably at me. Blue-eyed, wearing a backless white dress, she looked about nineteen, was dripping with money and exuded a soft, mischievous sexuality.

"Mr Halloran, I am delighted you are able to be here."

I tried not to stare down the front of her dress.

"Simon is in the library. I'm Davinia, his wife."

That disappointed me. It also surprised me. Either Lady Verity was older than she looked or this Verity character was a babysnatcher. She took my arm and navigated us through the crowded room and down a corridor where the party guests became progressively thinner on the ground. Sensible man, Verity. Not only did he have a gorgeous wife. He also had the wit to hide in comfort while the hooray Henry element occupied the designated areas.

At a Sheraton desk near the velvet-curtained windows, a man sat silently, brandy glass in hand. Smoke from his cigar spiralled into a thin haze around the only light in the room, cast from an anglepoise lamp on the desk. To his left a shadow moved. I stiffened slightly. Lady Davinia was still hanging on to my arm. I always stiffen at sudden movement in the dark. Whoever is doing the moving is usually up to no good.

The shadow moved into the light, materializing into a dark-haired, gazelle-like figure of a woman. She wore a dazzling, psychedelic silk number that split and plunged in all the right places. Black hair fell loosely over bare shoulders. Her jawline was delicate but petulant. Her eyes fixed on me, sizing me up. With what object in mind I had no idea. I returned the look with only one. But my mind often works that way.

The man at the desk waved me to a chair, Hepplewhite or similar uncomfortable vintage. No wonder they sat up straight in those days. The door closed and I realized Lady Davinia had left us.

"I'm Verity," the man announced. "My private secretary, Lucinda Bellamy."

La Bellamy handed me a man-sized Waterford of twelve-year-old malt. Hell, they even knew what I drank. I looked at Lucinda again and envied Verity one aspect of his job. The after hours' secretarial work looked worthwhile.

Verity stood up. A rotten trick, that — inviting a man to sit down then standing over him to address him like a public meeting. But it was a deliberate tactic on his part. He wanted me to feel disadvantaged. He had the physique of an Australian fast bowler and the face of a school swot. A lock of fair hair fell over his forehead and he swept it back into place with an almost effeminate gesture of his right hand. Then he drummed bony fingers on a beige folder that lay on the desk.

"I'll come straight to the point," he announced.

I looked in Lucinda's direction. He understood my meaning immediately because he said curtly:

"You can talk to Lucinda as you would to me. She has top Security clearance."

Wrong Verity. There were things I would say to Lucinda I would never say to you, if she gave me the chance.

"I'll come straight to the point," Verity repeated himself, as if going back to the beginning of a rehearsed script: "You knew Jack Lane."

I knew Jack Lane. But what was that to do with Verity?

"I worked with him some years ago," I replied.

Hell, I had done more than work with Jack. He had brought me up in the ways of the Omega Section. Before I met Jack I thought I was the best street man in the business. I wasn't, Jack was, by a bloody mile. He taught me everything he knew and he taught it well. Some of it had kept me alive in the intervening years. But as far as the outside world went, I worked with him some years ago.

"He's dead," Verity announced calmly and waited for my reaction. He didn't get one.

"I'd like you to read this report." He handed me the beige folder.

So that was the catch. Study on stress for the Home Office indeed. Ames said Verity had been at Omega Section records. So what was the bastard playing at? Only after thinking through these suspicions did I spare a thought for Jack Lane. But that was how well he had taught me. Self-preservation first.

Both Verity and Lucinda were studying my reaction.

"Poor old Jack," I commiserated and took a stiff slug of malt in memoriam.

"You hadn't heard?" Verity asked.

"No. I've been out of the country. So let's see what's in the paperwork."

They had buried Jack Lane on 23 January and had difficulty finding any mourners. Not that I would have gone, even for Jack. Mixing with dead people is not my idea of a social occasion. His ex-wife had attended, probably to check out it was a genuine excuse for his not keeping up with the alimony payments. Jack must have had a lousy lawyer: ex-wife living it up with some bright young thing from the B.B.C. and Jack paying for it. That must have stretched the apology for a salary they paid him as a Grade Three Security Officer with M.I.5. But that was the story of Jack's life in recent years.

When I first knew him he had been the best. Top man in the Omega Section. Things started to go wrong when his wife started playing around. Jack started drinking: not the occasional glass but the necessary tumblerful, usually before breakfast. Jack had always enjoyed a drink but operational he was teetotal. That changed. He took himself off assignments and on several occasions I found him legless in his office. Maybe the drink played on his already frayed nerves and that was why he lost his ability to cope with the rough stuff. He never did tell me and I never asked. He deserved to be left with his pride even if he did slide so far down the ladder he could scarcely remember where he had once stood. Eventually he got the drinking under some kind of control but his nerve had gone. Ames pulled strings to have him taken on by Five, more out of pity than anything else. Jack had been forty-seven when he cracked. If they could hide him in the system until his fifty-fifth birthday he could retire with some kind of pension.

Jack had not even made that. He was fifty-three.

Section Three of M.I.5 had compiled their report. It was their job to investigate any incident involving Security or Intelligence personnel and liaise with Special Branch at the Yard who were supposed to do the leg work. Section Three's recommendation would then be passed on to the top floor at Five, Directorate level. They usually checked someone had signed the report and would more often than not accept the recommendations without reading any further. So why had Verity got hold of it?

The thin brown folder contained not only Section Three's report but also a transcript of an inquest and a local police report. So I ignored my surroundings and settled down to read everything very carefully.

Chapter 3

Since his transfer to Five, Jack Lane's life had consisted of the dogsbody stuff, the routine deadbeat work that is the sorry lot of anyone unfortunate enough to be an S.O.3. Occasionally, Jack's section head threw him the odd bone in the shape of a routine base inspection, just to give him some fresh air. Jack had been on one of these rural jaunts when it happened.

On Friday 10 January, Jack had booked accommodation at the Lion Hotel in Glyntywyn, a West Wales county town, under his proper name and a bogus occupation: clerk at the Department of Health and Social Security. Jack had obviously not lost his sense of humour. He had visited the Experimental Weapons and Proof Testing Establishment at nearby Llanmartin to carry out a base inspection. He had filed an interim status report: 'A.O.K.' at 1800 hours Monday 13 January from the base.

The next thing Jack's control heard was from the local Special Branch liaison on Jack's home manor. The Glyntywyn police had been on to the local station looking for next-of-kin. Because Jack's name was on file at his local station as being a person of interest to Special Branch, they had been informed. It was therefore standard procedure for them to advise Jack's control.

The Glyntywyn police were blissfully unaware of Jack's real purpose in life and Five saw no reason to enlighten them. His I.D. card had been undiscovered, hidden in the lining of his suitcase which the appropriate 'relative', appointed to protect his cover, reclaimed from the Glyntywyn police. They had compiled a report on his death which was sent on to the plods on Jack's home manor. Five had purloined it from there.

This report had emanated from Glyntywyn Divisional Police Headquarters and was signed by a Superintendent J. C. Daniels.

Jack's car, a Chrysler Horizon, had been noticed at 2300 hours on Friday 17 January by a routine mobile patrol. The blue Horizon was parked in a roadside area favoured by mountain walkers on the Black Mountains some thirty miles from Glyntywyn. The mobile plods had recognized a 'foreign' registration and checked its antecedents by radio. The car had not been reported stolen. So the incident was logged in the nearby station's Occurrences Book.

At 0817 hours the following morning, Jack Lane's frozen body was discovered, dressed in jeans, shirt and thin showerproof anorak over vest and underpants, with plimsolls on light-socked feet. A local farmer had discovered the body while checking outlying sheep after a severely icy night following intermittent snow. Jack's driving licence was found in the car which had, by now, taken on significance. According to the Glyntywyn police report, enquiries led to the Lion Hotel. Adamson, its manager, stated Jack had settled his account and checked out at 0930 hours Thursday 16 January after buying an Ordnance Survey map at reception and expressing an interest in walking to the castle ruins at Eppynt Ddu. In the opinion of the police surgeon, Jack had fallen while walking, broken his leg and been unable to summon help or assist himself out of that high, lonely place. The snow had fallen late on Thursday night, heavily. The following day icy winds had turned it into a blizzard. The body had been discovered two miles from the nearest road. Time of death was estimated at very early Friday morning.

The Coroner's jury had dutifully followed the evidence, particularly the 'thorough' police report, commended to them by the Coroner and had returned a verdict of accidental death. The last gratuitous insult was the Coroner's pompous rider about the dangers inherent in being improperly equipped for mountain-walking trips. Presumably the entire court had then repaired to the nearest boozer, had a few large ones, and gone its component ways, everyone feeling smug and upright about having done their duty as honest citizens.

Attached to Section Three's report was a photocopy of the Llanmartin Base Security Report signed by Jack and dated Wednesday 15 January. It was Jack's signature all right and bore out the Base's statement that Jack had waved them farewell on the Wednesday night after completing the inspection and awarding a top-clearance grade. It was all very tidy.

Poor old Jack. He had lived the last five years of his life in a mess and had died very neatly. An ex-paratrooper more at home on a frozen hillside than in his own bedroom had gone mountain walking dressed like a spotty teenager on a school outing. Hell, Jack's training taught him to survive in the Arctic if he broke a leg. Whisky-sodden deadbeat he might have been, Jack could still have walked those two miles on his fingernails if he had to. Just supposing he was forced to remain relatively immobile, he had a knife with him. Jack would have grabbed one of those outlying sheep, cut its throat, eaten it raw, and wrapped himself in the fleece to stay alive. You had to be a hard man to survive as a para. You had to be even harder to contemplate being in the Omega Section. I did not buy it.

As a story it was better than anything from Hans Christian Andersen. Section Three had stamped the report; RECOMMEND NO FURTHER ACTION. They needed their arses kicking all the way down Whitehall.

Verity coughed, maybe to remind me he was still in the room.

"Neat paperwork," I observed, handing the report back to him.

In return I received the school-swot stare. Intense scrutiny. Never make the mistake of thinking these top civil servants sit on well-padded backsides, dreaming of inflation-proof pensions and letting the work slide. They are conspirators to a man. They can abort the politicians' wishes while procreating themselves to their own advantage. And when they play, it is only to win.

"Mr Halloran, I was told you are no fool."

"You were told the truth. And the truth of Jack Lane's death is not contained in that report. They'd make the Chief Rabbi Archbishop of Canterbury before Jack would die as the result of a fall on any mountain."

When he thought I wasn't looking, Verity shot Lucinda a quick glance. I was watching her. She was really beautiful.

"So what would be your recommendation?" Verity demanded.

"Send it back to Section Three and tell them to do a proper job."

"You're very sure of your ground."

"Goes with my job."

"Would you look into the matter, unofficially?"

He made the request sound matter-of-fact, as if he were asking me to see his secretary home. Jack Lane's voice was ringing in my ears now, hammering home one of the first rules of survival. "When the bastards want you to go unofficial, you're out on a limb. You're deniable. Never go unofficial, H. Never."

My mental processes were working overtime. What exactly was going on?

"Forget it," I replied. "Jack may have got slow and been an old piss artist but he was taken out by experts. In my view they rigged his death to look like one plausible accident. Anyone that good would probably eat one solitary Halloran stumbling around for a solution without recourse to official back-up."

I waited for his reaction. Verity smiled and appealed to my ego and any sense of loyalty I may have felt to Jack all at the same time.

"I was told you were a survivor, and a ruthless, unpleasant opponent. I also understand that you and Lane were once good friends."

"You don't have any friends in my line of work, just acquaintances," I replied.

"I heard a rumour recently," he came straight back at me: "that no-one kills an Omega Section operative and lives to brag about it. A sort of insurance policy to ensure the continued survival of the species? Apparently the Red Brigades killed Bradley in Rome some years ago. They considered it amusing. Then the late Mr Lane returned the compliment by removing Salvi and Amoro. Mr Scott was liquidated in Paris. It was your turn to take exception to that. I'm told you did, specifically on a top-notch Department Five K.G.B. hood. S.I.S. told me, somewhat enviously, that Mr Carmichael was released with many apologies and in one piece when those Basque people realized who he worked for. Had that been a Special Branch man or even an S.I.S. operative they would probably have tried to trade him. You put the fear of God into people, don't you? So what makes Jack Lane different? Surely not the fact that he was no longer with the section?"

Verity really wanted me on this one. He'd even dredged up that whispered rumour about us looking after our own. Well, it was more than a rumour. I knew I owed Jack Lane. But his telling me was an insult, especially since the most dangerous thing Verity had probably done was to make an improper suggestion to Lucinda.

"Tactically this is still a job for a policeman. Or send in the bloody cavalry. Special Branch, Section Three, Internal Security, the lot."

For a moment it looked as though Verity would go on the defensive. Instead he produced the usual winner. Reasons of state. And he made it sound very plausible. He even had the grace to concede me the point about tactics.

"I agree with your reasoning, Mr Halloran. But although there is nothing top secret scheduled for the Llanmartin Experimental Weapons Establishment, I'd rather not have size twelve feet trudging around the area. They tend to attract publicity and the next thing we know there will be a gypsy encampment of ululating unwashed women and misguided clergymen blocking the entrance."

I lit a cigarillo and finished my whisky. I could still hear Jack's voice telling me to refuse. Yet somewhere in the darkness I could feel his restless ghost, wandering aimlessly, calling the old war-cry of the Jack Lane I knew; a proud, upright man saying: "Come on, H. Time to go and nail the bastards."

"Does Ames know about this?"

"No. Officially you're assisting with this study on stress. I'd rather you kept it that way."

By now Verity could smell blood. I could almost hear his mental processes congratulating themselves. I said only:

"Where can I reach you?"

"Report any progress to Lucinda. If she is unavailable, here is my home telephone number."

He handed me a card. On his way out he said:

"Do enjoy the party."

Lucinda took a cigarette and waited for me to light it. I ignored the gold table lighter and used my own matches. She took the Waterford, refilled it, and poured herself some blue concoction in a very tall glass half full of ice.

Chanel perfume hung on the air and with it, another scent, the scent of power. There was a hard, ruthless streak in La Bellamy. I could read it in her wide brown eyes. Maybe that was why I found her attractive, apart from her other, more obvious, attributes. Yes, she would have to be ruthless to mix with the Veritys of this world. Natural stablemates, I guessed, from the same social background, a background that assumed power and responsibility, the professional power and influence brokers.

"If you need anything, let me know," she announced.

"How about you for starters?"

"You're presumptuous, Halloran."

Peasant put firmly in place. So I became curious.

"Are you sleeping with him?"

"If I am, it's none of your prurient concern." Her reply was cold, almost imperious.

Any moment now I expected the castle guard to march me to the dungeons. But she felt some kind of explanation was due. Or perhaps she realized I would get worse unless bought off with some scraps from the table.

"I have worked with Simon for two years. I am not sleeping with him. Davinia and I were at school together. You see, I introduced her to Simon."

And I'll bet you were the head girl. Where? Roedean? Steady Halloran, no more funny remarks. Learning time.

"Second wife," I observed. "So what happened to the first?"

"Ran off with the ski-instructor at Gstaad, two years ago."

"Beats getting laid by the milkman."

That remark did not go down at all well. The brown eyes flashed and I was made to feel like something unpleasant the cat had left on the Axminster.

"You ask a lot of questions," she observed, scathingly.

"Professional curiosity reinforced by a throwback to childhood. I once had a teacher who was always telling me to ask questions. Long time ago, of course, in the days when they had teachers."

Not quite true. Not so long ago. And Jack Lane had been a great teacher.

"And where did you go to school?" she asked.

"Nowhere you'd have heard of."

Then she switched to the attack with a very pertinent question. She asked it hoping I would be forced into a revealing answer that would give her a hint of weakness.

"Why retire, Halloran? Not losing your nerve, are you?"

"You ask a lot of questions too."

"I had a teacher once who told me the same thing, at Roedean. They still have teachers there."

Halloran made to feel like second-class citizen again.

"I'll bet you could teach me a thing or two, Lucinda."

She smiled, then the eyes turned hard.

"I doubt it. You look much too used-up."

There was some truth in that, although not, I suspected, in the sense that she meant. I asked her to lock the beige folder away and give me a key so I could retrieve it later. Then we joined the party and she disappeared into a throng.

Lady Davinia saw that I was alone. Like a good hostess she introduced me to the City's favourite whizz-kid-of-the-month. You know the guy: centrefold in the Business News. His girlfriend had front teeth like a Derby winner and whinnied at his appalling jokes. He asked me what I thought about the numbers of Unlisted Securities. I assumed he was talking about something else and tried to change the subject.

An hour later I was ready to go home. Good food, and the booze flowed like Verity had shares in it. But not my type of party. I didn't drive an Aston Martin, all I knew about the City was that it had its own police force, and when it came to foxhunting I was with the fox. I had been hunted before and I knew the feeling. Then a voice I knew said:

"Who let you in?"

It was Goldstein. Repulsive of appearance, his parents' fault: repulsive of manner, his own. The kind of Jew that makes Israelis anti-semitic, Goldstein masqueraded as some kind of journalist. Back in '67, during the rush to defend the Promised Land, Goldstein was rushing the other way. He spent his time pontificating about the righteousness of the Jewish cause while

21

sending its charities rubber cheques.

"Hello Goldstein, the ugly bug ball is down the road."

He ignored the insult and helped himself to a sandwich. I forgave the Israelis Goldstein because they also produced the best in the world — the Mossad.

"Those are pork," I advised. "The ones on your left are smoked salmon."

"While I have cause to be grateful for your existence, Halloran, I don't have to stay here to be insulted."

Goldstein drew himself up to his full five feet two and exuded crimson indignation.

"No," I agreed. "You could always go wherever it is you usually go to be insulted."

No-one at the party seemed to have any time for Goldstein either so we were an exclusive association of two, misfits in an otherwise socially compatible environment, to quote a university lecturer I once knew.

I had met Goldstein some years before. A rally for those who wanted Britain for the residents of Greater London able to prove ten generations of White Anglo-Saxon Protestant lineage had broken up early. And five hairless young morons were trying to break Goldstein up in some dark alley. I had just fingered some nutter the Italians wanted to extradite and was in the company of three hairy Special Branch lads when I noticed the squeaking shape of Goldstein being used for a football. Street thugs are at the same level as child molesters in my book so I led the charge. Seconds later there were five different footballs, snivelling and bleeding their way home to their unmarried mothers, minus bovver boots and trousers. I took Goldstein off to the nearest safe house and tidied him up. The poor guy had been scared witless as well as hurt. I suggested he forget the incident. Ever since, he has believed I'm some kind of bent copper and I don't have the heart to disillusion him.

Goldstein started rabbiting on about how good it was to see Verity happy again. I have always been a good listener, taking the wheat with the chaff. It's surprising how often extraneous information comes in very useful. Rowena, the Mark One wife, had left a lot to be desired. As Goldstein put it, there was quite a lot of her and quite a few people desiring it, including the ski-instructor at Gstaad. Verity's son had been badly injured in a car crash and was now a wheelchair case in some special hospital. But the final cruelty had occurred just before Christmas. Verity's stepdaughter, who had already flown the coop and lived in Europe, had fallen to her death after a seaside party. Good old Goldstein was like the speaking clock. Once dialled it continued ad nauseam in the same repetitive voice. I was sick of the virtues of Lady Davinia, about whom Goldstein obviously had secret fantasies. So I changed the subject to Lucinda Bellamy.

"Clever girl, Cambridge First, wealthy farming family from Hampshire. She used to live with some American attached to the Embassy here. Not any more, though. He was posted, as they say. You two would get on well together, Halloran. She too has the loving personality of a piranha fish. Be warned. She looks good enough to eat. She might just end up eating you."

Eventually I managed to lose Goldstein. I was tired, out of favour with the female of the species, and confused about Verity's motives for investigating Jack Lane's death. So I headed for the Library, key in hand, to unlock the file on Jack Lane. I would take it home with me and have a quiet wake on my own, in memoriam.

Chapter 4

IT DIDN'T WORK out that way. As I emerged from the library, file tucked underneath my arm, Lucinda Bellamy appeared from nowhere and threw her arms around me.

"Darling, I've been looking everywhere for you."

I thought my luck had miraculously changed. No. She had an ulterior motive. One irate hooray Henry was watching us. He deliberately ground out his cigar butt on the carpet and twisted the acrid mess further into the deep pile with his heel. I got the impression he was pretending it was my face.

"Look pleased to see me," she whispered.

So I kissed her. That was looking pleased to see her. Although she showed no outward signs of resistance, her whole body tensed, as if I was something that had just escaped from the snake house. Her pursuer had already stalked off but I wasn't letting on. I kissed her again and detected an easing of the tension. But she stiffened again when I ran my fingers down her bare spine. She broke off the kiss.

"Okay, Halloran. He's gone. Escort me to the door, will you. Simon's chauffeur is driving me back to Town."

"He can drive me as well. Hold on to the paperwork. Your friend is bigger than I am. I might need two hands."

"So long as they're only for fending Charles off."

The butler helped Lucinda into her coat. We walked across the gravel to meet the Rolls. Regrettably, Charles had got there before us. In the pale yellow outside light he looked bigger than I first thought. In fact, he was bloody enormous. I am six feet tall, well almost, and weigh just over twelve stone. Charles was four inches taller, four stone heavier and ten years younger. And for a drunk, he was remarkably steady on his feet. He was also persistent.

"Lucinda, darling," he slurred in best Harrovian. "Come with Charlie."

He allowed her to pass then blocked my way. The ease with which some people escalate violence sometimes frightens me. Because they don't really have the first idea of what it is all about. Charles had decided he wanted to be a big man and show off to the girls. I didn't want to know it.

"I don't like you," he muttered loudly. "You're a right Wally."

Insults I can take. Threats to my person, never. Charles lurched at me. I always avoid drunken brawls and never mix in domestic arguments on principle. But Charles wanted to use me for a punchbag to show what a big brave boy he was. Prat. He leaned back to take a swing at me. I didn't give him the chance to do anything else.

My right knee drove hard into his groin. Rule One: Always get the first blow in. As he doubled forward I pulled his fat head down on to my knee which was following through, hard. He yelped in blind pain as his nose spread all over his face. The blood spurted. Then I kicked his right kneecap, hard. Rule Two: Hit the bastard in three places at the same time.

He doubled on the ground, clutching his squashed testicles and wailing about his bleeding face. I joined Lucinda in the Rolls. Rule Three: Never wait around after a brawl. Your assailant might have friends who want to restore his reputation. And you have to be lucky to win against more than one man. That only happens on the films. They might also tell it different from how it was. And if a policeman can charge anyone, it makes his journey worthwhile, irrespective of the rights and wrongs of the situation.

"On, James," I ordered the chauffeur.

Lucinda looked severely at me.

"That was vicious," she remonstrated. "He didn't even hit you."

"Anyone making a hostile move towards me has forfeited his civil rights. You wanted an escort, Charlie wanted to fight. You both got what you wanted. Stop complaining and pour me a whisky."

"Very macho," she snapped, handing me the drink.

I lit a cigarillo and took a stiff pull at the booze. My stomach settled down and my hands stopped shaking. No matter how much aggravation I dealt with, the after-effects were always the same.

"Who was he?"

"Why, Halloran? You want to pay him a visit and really do the job? That's you, isn't it? I know all about you. They call you the Headhunter, the number one nasty. You shouldn't be let out."

"Keep savage pets and complain when the training is put to use. I broke his nose and injured his reproductive chances for one reason. If he had floored me, I might not have got up again. He had the choice of backing down or being carried out. Not old Harrovian manners, I admit. But you probably haven't noticed: there is no room for second chances out on the streets. Jack Lane would tell you that."

"Psychopath."

I ignored the remark. But she would not leave it alone. Women are like that. One of their least attractive qualities: give them cause for complaint and they are like a dog with a bone. They go back, dig it up again and worry it.

"I don't like you. You're arrogant, violent and chauvinistic."

"Just like Charles. More whisky please." I held my glass out.

She poured herself a drink and maintained an aloof silence. But it was all an act. She had derived some satisfaction from seeing Charles beaten to a pulp. She just didn't want to admit it. Yes, there was definitely a hard, ruthless streak in La Bellamy.

The chauffeur obviously knew where Lucinda lived without being told. He was probably going to get his revenge on me by leaving me on the Dilly. Halfway along a row of Georgian houses near Sloane Square, the Rolls slowed down.

"This is where I leave you," she told me. "I won't ask you in for coffee."

Which was the last thing on my mind. I held on to her arm and ordered the chauffeur to drive on, turn out of sight and come back up the street the opposite way.

"What the hell for?" Lucinda demanded.

I was not listening. I was too busy watching the dark Sierra parked among other cars opposite the Bellamy abode. There were three men in that car. They might have been cops. On the other hand they might not have been. One of them noticed us going by the second time. By now Lucinda had realized something was wrong. I noted the registration number and reached for the car phone. She looked directly at me and her hand gripped mine.

I glanced back to see if the Sierra was following us.

"Duty officer." The voice on the other end of the line sounded suitably bored.

"Blue One," I announced, using my call sign. That woke the bastard up. "Check out the following vehicle and call me at the Alamo."

I relayed the registration and location of the Sierra, together with a vague description of its contents. Then I put the receiver back where it belonged. The chauffeur had heard Alamo and so had Lucinda.

"You'll never get in there," she predicted confidently.

The chauffeur must have thought so. He took a short cut and within minutes pulled up outside the place where the beautiful people dine and disco. We did get in. I was always welcome at the Alamo because I knew Sean who owned it. He insisted that I saved his life in Vietnam but we never talk about it because I was never supposed to have been in Vietnam.

At a corner table in the quietest of the three bars, Lucinda chose whisky. So I ordered the proper malt, told the waiter to leave the bottle but put the contents on Sean's account. For the first time since we had met, Lucinda smiled at me as though she meant it.

"Say this for you, Halloran, you really are good."

"Some have said the best. But they listen to a lot of gossip. Why would anyone be watching your flat?"

"I have no idea," she laughed.

"You're not having it away with someone else's husband who has put private detectives on to you?"

"Don't be so inquisitive."

I gripped her arm, tightly.

"Don't play about with me, darling. This isn't charades at the bloody Dorchester now. This is for real."

I probably sounded angry. Because I was angry. Heavy men in my slipstream was a serious business. Then Lucinda's brown eyes were all wide and innocent and she said quietly:

"I don't know who they are, Halloran. Honestly."

I let go of her arm. Maybe she was telling me the truth. I poured us two more whiskies. No way was I going to fight anyone else tonight. Which was why I had called in about the Sierra. So I lit two cigarillos for us and sat back in relative comfort.

"It's too late for a hotel," I observed. "So unless you know anyone well enough to wake them at this hour and demand sanctuary, you had better come home with me."

"Halloran, I've seen some try-ons in my time. But for sheer subtlety, yours beats them all."

"You could always walk the streets."

That suggestion was not appreciated.

An androgynous waiter approached, placed a cordless phone on the table and smiled suggestively at me. I scowled back. Someone

27

ought to have a word with Sean about him. The call was from the duty officer who wasn't happy.

"Those three in the Sierra were Internal Security. What are you trying to do, H? Start a war?"

"Who sent them?"

"They told Special Branch to piss off. I don't have the authority to force the issue. If you want explanations, that's down to you."

I put the phone down on him. Internal Security — Rigby's mob, the people who watched the watchers and sent cold shivers down clandestine spines. But they weren't allowed to operate on the Omega Section. Not since the aforementioned Carmichael took a pot shot at one of them. The idiot Carmichael was no longer with us. But neither were Internal Security. Either they were watching Lucinda, or the ubiquitous Rigby was bending the rules. I finished my whisky.

"Way past my bedtime, Lucinda. Come along."

I had already sent the Rolls home to Verity. Too conspicuous for travelling around in when the watchers were about. We took a cab. No-one followed us.

I lived out of that familiar suitcase mostly and at the time it was resting in a basement flat off the Earls Court Road. Lucinda was holding my hand as we descended the darkened steps. Suddenly, an unnatural yell split the night air. Lucinda hung on tight to my arm. I realized what had happened, but not before my pulse rate had leaped alarmingly. I had trodden on that damned cat again. As I opened the door I felt a shape brush my leg and vanish into the flat.

"Clumsy feline," I cursed.

Lucinda relaxed her grip and giggled.

I rented the place furnished from a bent antique dealer I knew. The décor was late Victorian, early grotesque, with authentic rising damp to give it that genuine condemned look. The bedroom was dry enough but it had only one bed. Lucinda inspected the premises and announced sarcastically:

"Very chic. You get the sofa."

"I get the bed. You can have half. The machine wakes me up and makes coffee. Don't feel you have to bring me breakfast. I can rarely face it."

"You've got the brass neck of — "

"Drink that." I handed her a glass of the duty free malt. Customs never ask me if I have anything to declare when I'm operational. Considered bad form. Lucinda put her feet up on the sofa. I noticed the slit in her dress revealed bare leg up to her left thigh. Provocation. She noticed my eyes wandering and realized the cat had joined us.

"What do you call your cat?"

The cat looked at the gas fire. I lit the appliance. The cat stretched out in the warmest place.

"Not my cat. Not anybody's cat. He turned up on the doorstep two days after I moved in. Sometimes answers to the name of Moshe Dayan."

She tried calling him. Moshe Dayan ignored her. Instead he opened his one good eye and looked at me with a self-satisfied grin on his evil face. He'd been out on the town, tomming it again.

"Not very prepossessing, is he?"

"What you might call a working cat," I explained. "Fights a lot. That's why there are bits missing out of his ears. Hair on his head is thinning. Sign of old age. He gets by all right. I suppose he's like me. We respect each other's privacy."

"Do you feed him?"

"Sometimes, if he asks."

Moshe Dayan didn't. He knew he was being talked about. He never took kindly to strangers and considered humanity a foolish species. Ignoring Lucinda's calls, he stretched himself again and closed his one good eye.

Just then I took my jacket off and Lucinda noticed my gun. Interest flickered in those brown eyes and she asked:

"Do you always carry that?"

"Often."

"It looks big enough to stop an elephant. May I?"

I unloaded the revolver and handed it to her, butt first. She looked at it, weighed it in both hands, and levelled it, double-handed, at the doorway. Then she squeezed the trigger.

"Don't do that," I ordered.

You should never squeeze a trigger on an empty chamber. It jars the firing pin. And while the rule applies mostly to shotguns and hammerless weapons, a rule is a rule — especially where firearms are concerned.

"Smith & Wesson .41 Magnum," she announced. "Never heard of this before."

There was nothing clever in her identification. She could read it engraved on the metalwork. My .41 had a four-inch barrel. Lighter than its much-vaunted big brother, the .44 Magnum, the world's most powerful handgun, it still packed a tremendous punch. I handloaded my own shells heavily enough to stop dead anything on two legs but not heavily enough to make the recoil, and therefore the second shot, uncomfortable. Consequently I had more stopping power than with a .357 Magnum and so much more than with the regulation issue .38 Special that my artillery made the copper's friend look like something that inflicted gnat bites.

"Have you ever killed anyone with this?" Lucinda asked.

"I only carry it to hide my tailor's mistakes."

What tailor? On the money I was paid I couldn't afford a hand-made handkerchief. It was time to talk about something else rather than guns. I reclaimed the forty-one and holstered it.

"I'm going for a shower, then bed. Switch the light off after you."

"Yes, O Master," she teased.

Somehow all this was unreal. Internal Security watching Lucinda's flat, her boss wanting me to go unofficial, and both of us sinking too much whisky in the small hours.

Once in the bedroom I reloaded the forty-one and jammed it, in its holster, between the mattress and the bed base, right-hand side, butt outward. I could get to it fast in that position. Never leave a gun under the pillow. You either blow your own ear off or nasty accidents occur if you're lucky enough to have an energetic sleeping companion. Anyway, a night's sleep is impossible with several pounds of metal under your head.

I threw the bedspread back over the gun butt and went in to the shower. The hot spray of water on top of too much whisky gave me a warm, easy feeling. My thoughts drifted towards sex with Lucinda. But I expected she was seeking material for an Iron

Curtain of a bolster to go in the bed.

I had to pinch myself because I didn't believe it was happening. The shower curtain moved and I was joined by an active brunette with long legs and firm young flesh. Lucinda pushed me away from the spray and giggled. I slipped and came up at breast level.

"I came to rub your back," she whispered.

"That's not my back you're rubbing."

Then she stood back, legs apart, hands on slim hips, water streaming over her wet hair. The brown eyes mocked. She started teasing.

"Not gay, are you?"

"If I was, you've converted me."

"You can rub my back now."

She turned around and moved very close, her shoulders arched and she bent forward.

"Keep doing that," she moaned, "yes, yes, ye . . . es."

I wasn't rubbing her back, either.

Chapter 5

I DID NOT sleep. I should have done because I was exhausted. By the time Lucinda was sleeping softly and maybe dreaming it was 6.15 am. Idly stroking the magnificent curve of her naked back, I wondered why it had been my lucky night. I try very hard with the ladies, but Valentino I am not. My slept-in face and diminishing hair don't match that image.

Women have a reason for everything they do or don't do. Women like Lucinda in particular. She might have been crazy about sex in the showers, or sex on the floor, or just sex anywhere. Somehow I didn't think that was her sole motive for sleeping with me. Annoying thing about women. They are almost impossible to read.

I made coffee and livened it up with a shot of blended whisky. My throat was dry and furry. Then I thought about Jack Lane again and re-read the file Verity had given me. One thing was missing. I had noticed it the night before but I did not intend letting on to Verity. I reckoned he had a head start in the matter without me opening my big mouth.

Standard procedure: Five had inventorized the contents of Jack's office desk and his flat. But they had failed to discover his gun. And if that was missing, odds were he had gone down to Wales expecting trouble. You don't expect trouble on routine base inspections.

Officially Jack was not supposed to have a gun. Which explained why Five were not heartbroken at the lack of one. Jack's Ministry permit to carry had been revoked the day he left the Omega Section. It had been my job to see he handed that permit in. The gun was his own affair. I remembered him saying: "Stuff surrendering the hardware. You never know when you might need an untraceable gun."

So at 7.25 am I celluloided my way into Jack's flat. I was looking for a Browning GP35 automatic in 9mm Parabellum. Old regulation issue. Jack was a conservative when it came to guns. He was used to the Browning from Army days. It carried thirteen rounds and Jack liked to have enough ammunition immediately available. And Jack was an expert with that Browning.

Five had been through the flat already, leaving most things just as they had found them. Jack's personal paperwork was fairly tidy even if I did have to move the whisky bottles to get at it. His recent history was all there: money wasted on booze, lawyers' correspondence and exorbitant fee notes, documents relating to the sale of the house, and the proceeds from his share he hadn't got round to drinking. Going through the stuff I felt guilty. I had to admit that he really did have feet of clay. I had not been around much to help him. You don't have friends in my line of work. But in those early years, Jack had been the closest I had come to having one.

The remainder of the flat was much as he had left it, although the woman who slept there sometimes had recently tidied it up for him. The perfume in the bathroom and the photo in the bedroom both belonged to a familiar face, a well-preserved redhead called

Annette. They had this on-off thing going since Jack's marriage broke up.

I looked in all the usual hiding places. There was no gun. Which meant the next stop had to be Harry's.

His premises were in the nether regions behind Portobello Road. Harry was a bent general dealer whose left hand never knew what the right was doing so his tongue would never embarrassingly loosen in the presence of the Law. Harry was the very spirit of the free-enterprise economy. He obtained his gear mostly free and sold it for an enterprising price. Aged fifty, a bespectacled, humble, creeping form of what passed for humanity, Harry continually wore a tatty suit that must have been rejected for demob issue back in 1946.

I spotted the suit superintending removals from a furniture van. Washing machines, probably described on a fake invoice as war-damaged goods from Iran. I tapped a rounded shoulder. A head inclined nervously. Rodent features looked sideways at me.

"Don't do that," he protested, swivelling eager eyes back again to watch the unloading and ensure he was not short-delivered: "I thought you was Old Bill."

"I'm old Halloran. Where's Jack Lane's Browning?"

He steered me swiftly into his workshop.

"Keep yer voice down. Back in a minute."

It took five. Harry locked the doors, paid off the delivery men and stuffed more money than I earned in a month back into an inside pocket.

"Cup of tea, Mr H?"

I glanced around at the encrusted gas ring, battered kettle, chipped, stained mugs and the curdled milk. The whole place smelled unpleasant, a stale, abused smell. The environmental health would have condemned it. They would most likely have condemned Harry as well, flushed everything down a treatment works and disinfected the lot.

"Jack's gun," I demanded.

Harry's rodent eyes swivelled again, bright at the thought of turning my request into a profit. He knew better, but that didn't stop him trying.

"What gun would that be, Mr H?"

"Harry. Would you like Old Bill round for that cup of tea?"

He visibly recoiled.

Whatever else Harry might be, he was a first-rate armourer. On occasions I had trusted him to do some work for me. He had learned his trade with the Army. Then they discovered he was running his own selling business using their stock. They pointed out that the Ministry of Defence Sales did not want inside competition. Harry was thrown into the glasshouse.

"GP35 Browning," Harry recalled instantly. "Lovely piece of work. Accurized, no serial numbers. A craftsman's gun that."

"Where is it?"

"Mr Lane's got it. I overhauled it for him not long back. Rush job, he said."

"When was that?"

"What's this about?" Harry became very defensive.

"Jack Lane is no longer with us. They did not send the gun back with the rest of him."

Harry's eyes swivelled upwards this time. A silent prayer to the Great Armourer in the sky. Harry began to perspire. He always perspired at the thought of comebacks. Then came the excuses:

"Look, all I did was look at the gun, about three weeks back. I don't want aggro off anyone. If I tell you, leave me out of it with Old Bill. Please."

"Strictly between ourselves. Exact date?"

He consulted a tea-stained ledger, buried beneath a pile of pornography.

"January the ninth."

He closed the ledger and smiled humbly. Then:

"I say, Mr H. Don't suppose you'd be interested in some adult movies . . . ?"

By 9.45 I was back at my flat. A note from Lucinda read: "Thank you for having me. Call anytime. P.S. I've fed Moshe Dayan."

Memories of lithe limbs and warm flesh came flooding back. I dialled the number. No reply. Moshe Dayan looked up from where he was sitting with a superior cat-like expression on his battered face. Maybe he knew something I should but was just acting smug. I put him outside. He could go somewhere else and be smug. He stared indignantly at me for three seconds then disappeared.

I had one more call to make in the local search for Jack Lane's Browning. It was a long way out to Willesden looking for Annette, especially to find she had gone out. A neighbour told me she worked check-out in the local supermarket Saturdays. So I joined the queue of happy families, squawking brats, rampant children full of hot breakfast cereal and elderly shoplifters. Ten-pound note and can of beans clutched in my left hand, I stood at the check-out.

"Haven't you got anything smaller?"

"Than what, a can of beans?"

Annette looked up and did not smile. Her sad eyes demanded to know why I was standing there and Jack was dead. She said nothing.

"We need to talk."

Her fingers drummed nervously on the till.

"Cafe around the corner. I get a break in half an hour," she sighed, reluctantly.

On the way out a demented toddler rammed me with a supermarket trolley. Its long-suffering mother, with three more kids in tow, smiled apologetically. A fracas broke out at the door between a harassed, shirt-sleeved young man and a grey-faced pensioner. The inevitable blue uniforms loomed up. Bust of the week. They had caught one of the elderly shoplifters. Scenes from urban life.

The coffee was barely drinkable. I had tasted worse but not that year. Annette arrived on time, mac thrown over the supermarket overall, a cigarette held between nervous fingers. The lines around her eyes were more definite than I remembered, the hands rougher, the voice harder. Forty-six years old, faded immeasurably by the grief or was it only the years?

"He's dead, you know. So where were you? Not at the bloody funeral. That smiling bitch of a wife — "

"Somewhere else," I interrupted the torrent of recriminations, "doing what Jack used to. I found out yesterday. Annette, I am sorry."

"You look it. Come to pick over the bones, have you?"

It was pointless trying to dissuade her from bitterness. Maybe she was justified. All I wanted was information.

"Jack's gun. Where is it?"

"What's it to you?"

"Where, Annette?"

"I don't bloody well know. Took it with him, I expect. The big stupid sod was all I had. You bastards even had to take that away from me. You used him."

"How?"

She had not heard the question. Or then again she had and was ignoring it. Recriminations again. It was time to be a good listener.

"He was full of it, the night before he left. He made love to me, Halloran, and he was heroic. 'I've got a real job at last,' he said. 'Just like the old days. What I'm good at. No more shuffling the paperwork or ignoring the pitying looks. A top man wants me. This is my big chance.' Big chance? Someone bloody killed him. Then they covered it up."

"Did Jack put a name to this man?"

"No. And he hadn't touched a drop for three days. That's all I know. Piss off."

I held on to her scrawny arm.

"Anyone else been to see you?"

"No-one. Let go of me."

I released my grip. She pulled her arm away and almost knocked the coffee cup over. I gave her a cigarillo and watched a tear form in each sad eye. Sullenly defiant she said:

"He was proud to be asked, Halloran."

I took my wallet out and left all the notes I had on the table.

"Don't offer me charity," she hissed.

"Not charity. Buy him some flowers, or whatever."

I left the money where it was and walked out. She was still staring vacantly into the empty coffee cup.

I know the system inside out. Which enabled me to make another enquiry without anyone noticing. Jack's official papers were still in the garret-like offices down Clerkenwell way, in the grey warren where the S.O.3s hid out. On my own authority I could inspect any offices inside Five except Operations and the Top Floor without signing any chits to say I had done so.

The janitor took one look at my Blue Pass and opened up immediately. Thinking it was a spot check on building security and efficiency he explained they had not yet cleared Jack's desk. There was a go-slow among the civilian transportation staff in Documents. I'll swear that if the four-minute warning comes some fool will refuse to broadcast it. And probably because the wording hasn't been agreed at a lengthy inter-union conference taking a week at some five-star hotel. All the paperwork was tidy. Too tidy for Jack. He was the kind of man who left jottings on everything to remind him of life's important tasks: pay the rates, send mother-in-law an unpleasant present, remember the odd phone number you shouldn't have.

Going over Jack's desk really was picking over the bones. The memories came back, of the dirty jobs we had hacked together, the bars we had frequented off-duty, the promises we had made ourselves about finding an easier way to earn a living. But part of Jack was missing from that desk. The untidy part. Because all the paperclips were in a neat little tray. The desk diary was written up, duly inspected by his Section Head and countersigned on 9 January. The usual scraps of paper were missing. I couldn't find any beermats with doodles all over them. Although the janitor's log denied any official inspection I knew someone had been through the stuff before me. So who had sanitized the place? Internal Security? And what for?

Then I noticed the cigarettes. Nothing unusual about a crushproof pack of Marlboro except that Jack did not smoke. Four cigarettes had gone yet the pack looked like it had been carried around in someone's pocket for a while. I tipped the contents out on the desk and looked inside, between the silver paper and the cardboard. The hiding place had Jack Lane's trademark all over it. The slip of paper was two inches long by an inch wide. Jack had written a telephone number on it. I put it back in the pack with all the cigarettes and pocketed the pack.

Half an hour later I was in a nearby pub, a pint of lager to hand. Instinct told me it was all very dodgy. I was due to retire at the end of the month. Topmost drawer civil servant checks my record then requests me to go unofficial under cover of some study on stress. Lovely Lucinda and I screw each other all night. Internal Security dodging around. Jack Lane's Browning missing. And the telephone number Jack had carefully hidden was the same one Sir Simon Verity had given me to contact him outside office hours.

It seemed Jack Lane's ghost was trying to tell me something.

Chapter 6

I COULDN'T SUMMON up any enthusiasm for cooking. There was nothing in the flat I could cook, apart from that can of beans. So lunch was King Prawn Chow Mein from the local Chinese takeaway. Washed down with a lonely bottle of Sam Smith's Best Yorkshire Ale rescued from the refrigerator, it was a substantial meal. Moshe Dayan thought so too.

The villainous black psychic had been on the doorstep to greet me. He knew I had been to the Chinese. His one seeing eye gleamed expectantly. For good measure he sat on his haunches, alert, looking wistfully at my plate, making me feel like a sated pig rooting in a famine zone while the inhabitants starved. I threw him a prawn.

"Pay attention, cat. I'm away for a while."

He licked his lips, gave a small cry and caught the next prawn in mid-air. I'd have given my eye teeth for reactions that fast.

"Keep an eye on the place, from the outside. And don't talk to any strange men . . . or women."

He acknowledged the instruction with a small cry. Well, I thought he had acknowledged the instruction. He might have been asking for what was left of lunch. Damned cat. I never knew what he was thinking. I lived in a world where it was almost impossible to know what everyone was thinking. And it had been my luck to get mixed up with a cat who caused me the same problem. So I put the plate down for him. By the time I came back with my suitcase, the plate was clean. I locked the back door behind me, took my eyes off him for a second, and Moshe Dayan was no longer there. He had the right idea.

No-one from Internal Security or anywhere else followed me. I was making sure of that. I walked for two streets, took a taxi as far as Baker Street then walked again. Streetcraft. No-one would discover my real destination by talking to cabbies. I doubled back on my own tracks twice, entered shops by one entrance and left by another, stopped to look in shop windows, noted the looks in the eyes of passing pedestrians.

Eventually I registered under another name in a small, frayed hotel not far from Crawford Street. The bogus identity was to satisfy nosey callers. The proprietor knew me as Halloran, and well enough to provide a room containing a direct phone line without asking any damn fool questions. I paid the bill in advance, with used tenners from the emergency float I always kept hidden in my flat. The additional gratuity was for advance warning of any enquiries concerning me. Not that the transaction would go through any books. The proprietor cheated on his income tax. Like he said. They only take it away from you and waste it on bureaucrats' wages.

The room was clean, if spartan, the furniture unfashionable yet substantial. I stopped long enough to hang a 'Do not disturb' notice on the door handle, lock the room from the inside, and exit via the fire escape for some necessary shopping. It was dark when I returned to make the essential phone calls. By now I was very tired but my brain kept asking me questions I could not yet answer. It took half a bottle of Scotch to get me to sleep. I deserved the peace. I had gone to a lot of trouble not to be disturbed.

I woke up midday on Sunday. The cleaner had started vacuuming the landing. A late breakfast was sent up to the room. Then I left, again via the fire escape. I had paid for three nights' undisturbed rest.

By four pm I was driving across the Chiswick flyover in a 2.3

litre Cortina that looked like the typical company car it really was. I had obtained my own cover — those essential phone calls — and that cover would stand up to all but the most detailed examination. I was not anticipating trouble of that kind. I had not told Verity, Lucinda or even old Ames where I was going.

I had become Jeremy Hall, senior representative for a chemical cleaning supply company. In my recently-purchased three-piece suit I looked the part, even down to the slightly expanded waistline. I had dodged the last two training courses. Always look and act your cover.

Jeremy Hall was married, with two point four children, mortgaged detached house in Croydon and an overdraft at the bank. The last part was true. The best cover contains an element of fact. Driving licence, family photo of wife Charlotte, children Justin and Samantha, together with Biggles the family Labrador, nestled in my wallet. I didn't go much on Biggles or the kids but Charlotte was worth inviting round. Business and credit cards nestled with that happy snap in one half of the leather wallet. The other half contained a slimline pocket calculator with built-in alarm and executive game. The company which owned the car was bona fide and the Managing Director would field any enquiries about me. I had once done him a personal and unofficial favour, scotching industrial espionage. Now it was his turn.

Rep's cover was ideal for being curious about localities and people. Reps hung around in hotel bars, listened to gossip, chatted up the women, were pushy and got themselves noticed. Which would cover my real reason for going to Glyntywyn. I was looking for Jack Lane's Browning. Whoever had it must have been at least in part responsible for writing him off. So I would return the compliment, for and on behalf of. I had already promised Jack's ghost that much.

I was capable of it. When it was all over I would still be standing up. I had mixed it with the best of them in my time and was still in one piece — mostly. The I.R.A., Baader-Meinhof, Black June, the U.V.F., the spoilt little rich kids rejecting Daddy's values but not his money, the fashionable campus terrorists had all had their chances. I had even dented the edges of the K.G.B.

In return I had two bullet holes in me, one stab wound, and had broken most of my ribs at one time or another. I was thirty-eight years old, really too old to go mixing it with fit youngsters, but I was alive. And Lucinda Bellamy had been correct. The boys who knew the game called me the Headhunter. And this last assignment was not for Verity, my employers the government, or even for Ames. It was for my old and neglected one-time partner, Jack Lane.

I drove through misty darkness via Usk and Abergavenny, following the A40 towards Brecon — the old drovers' trail taken over first by the stagecoaches then by the motorist. Winding through the hills and watching my speed on glistening wet roads I realized I had not been there in fifteen years. The Parachute Regiment Battle School was at Dering Lines, to the east of the town. I remembered that far-away night in the Mess when Townshend Forbes won four cases of champagne after declaring loudly he could walk the Severn Bridge by its suspension cable and doing just that. Another ghost. A Paddy had shot him in the back from the cover of the Divis Flats and a mass of rioting schoolchildren. There were forty-seven pubs in Brecon in those days. We had been drunk in most of them. One I wanted to visit again. Because Jack Lane was an ex-para. And to ex-paras of his generation the Blue Bell was a spiritual home.

Frank was a small, grey, receding character who rarely saw the daylight. He looked like he was carrying mankind's troubles on his permanently-sloped shoulders. I doubted whether he was ever sober. The half-pint tankard would begin the evening as beer and end up seventy per cent vodka. He had kept the Blue Bell for twenty years. In turn it had kept him away from his wife, who never went near the bar except to demand money for clothes, Continental holidays and bingo. The pub was Frank's escape, his own world where he kept good beer, tolerated no tearaways, and watched other men's folly through late-night vision while silently conscious of his own failings.

The lounge was quiet. Only four pairs of eyes followed me to the bar.

"Long time." Frank grinned, the face older and tighter than I

41

remembered. I probably looked older, too.

"Thought you were dead," he muttered.

"Not yet, Frank."

"Got you a room, as requested."

"See you later."

A girl showed me upstairs; a big, square-jawed, broad-shouldered lass who looked at me as if I was breakfast. I tested the double bed.

"Very comfortable, I can tell you," she announced in a rasping Merthyr accent.

"I'm sure it is."

She said something uncomplimentary in Welsh. I replied in Welsh and she looked surprised. Then mercifully I was alone. I did not feel like explaining to her that I spoke Gaelic, Arabic, French and German and that my late mother had been brought up near Llandeilo.

I slept for a few hours. Then at three am I heard the bolts being locked in place downstairs and knew that the last paying drunk had gone home. Frank was in the lounge, gazing into the dying embers of the log fire. I poured myself a whisky and enjoyed it.

"Paddies didn't get you, then?" Frank raised his tankard.

"Not quite."

"Out of the blue, after all these years, you phone me. Yes, Jack Lane was through here."

"And?"

"Said he was on holiday, asked me what I knew about Glyntywyn. He was drinking tomato juices. Very unlike Jack. Next I heard was the report in the paper, on the inquest. Not like Jack to go out on the hills unprepared. Not like Jack to say he'll call back and then not turn up, either. Wonder what really happened. You're interested, I take it."

"Yes."

"What exactly are you doing these days, Halloran?"

"Selling."

"If you say so." He smiled inwardly. "Jack was curious about who ran Glyntywyn: personalities, police, local mafia. I told him what I knew which wasn't much. I referred him to a mate of mine,

Bill Islwyn Evans who keeps the Swan there. Bill phoned me a few days later, asked me not to send anyone else looking for news."

"Yet you're telling me, knowing that I'll most likely call with him."

"I liked old Jack. What happened to him isn't my affair. But if you're interested it means you've a good reason. I'll tell you what I told him. I don't want to get involved. I just run a pub."

Understandable attitude from one of life's observers. Frank was like just about everyone else in the world. He wanted to be left alone to get on with doing what he usually did.

"Glyntywyn itself is a county town," he began. "Agricultural area with some good businesses in the town. Holiday resorts dotted around extensive coastline. Now for the hearsay. Remember this is Wales, Halloran, where everyone minds everyone else's business. The crime is mainly gas meter stuff. The Glyntywyn police are holy terrors for the breathalyser but only from some pubs. In charge is a right bastard of a divisional super who rules with an iron rod bent in favour of the local controlling interest. Any publican who crosses him might as well close down. That might explain Bill's current attitude."

"Would that copper go by the name of J. C. Daniels?"

"Someone's marked your card already. Jack did ask me about a man named Garth Gwyn. Don't know or know of him but I have heard the local controlling interest is owned by the Gwyn family."

Frank didn't know any more. So he cooked me bacon and eggs for an early breakfast. Before I left I asked him to lock something up in his safe for me until I called to collect it. He was doubtful about minding my .41 Magnum. I was more doubtful about being caught in possession of it by the Glyntywyn police. That would really blow a very big hole in my cover.

I was on my way before dawn. I had reckoned on Jack showing his face at the Blue Bell. Now it was a question of following in his footsteps until I had the answer. Like I told Verity, it was really a job for a policeman, and I was no detective.

Dawn had broken by the time I drove up the climbing, winding road to that part of the mountains where Jack's body had been found. I had pinpointed the exact spot on an O.S. map. I stopped the car in the same gravelled parking area where his car had been discovered. The place was set back from the road a hundred yards, screened by fir trees that sheltered in the cleft of two hills. A mountain stream rushed noisily down that cleft and through a culvert running under the road. No passing police car would have noticed Jack's vehicle. It would have to drive on to the gravelled area then round a dog leg screened by those fir trees to notice a parked car. That Friday night police patrol must have pulled well off the highway, probably for a crafty smoke.

I climbed the hills and looked eastward. All I could see was short-grassed, grey-green outcropped limestone hill country. The edge of the Black Mountains. The keen wind stung my face. I felt like I was standing on top of the world, at the mercy of unnamed forces. I looked westward towards the road, for reassurance of Man's existence. The green patchwork quilt of the fertile Tywyn valley lay miles below.

I walked on. The open, desolate landscape despised overfed, centrally-heated, urban-dwelling man. It belonged to the elements: biting wind that chilled the soul, driving rain that drenched the spirit. Jack Lane understood country like this. In a curious way I knew it respected him. Years before we had walked the Brecon Beacons together. Jack and mountains were linked by some inexplicable spiritual bond. Even as a young soldier he was always climbing, anywhere he could: his stories about the Cairngorms, Snowdonia, Norway, the Alps and once the Himalayas were endless.

Jack would have been at one with this place. In its turn, it would have been neither bad-mannered nor ungrateful enough to kill him. For a moment up there I felt the wind whistling its denial of any involvement and the spirits of the place scorning that inquest verdict on a brother's death.

I walked back to the car telling myself to deal in facts and not some fancied spiritual experience. For some crazy reason I remembered Hamlet who said:

'There are more things in Heaven and Earth, Horatio, than are dreamt of in your philosophy.' Maybe I hadn't got it exactly and

44

literally correct, but that was the rough idea. Then I remembered some more Hamlet. Something like:

'The play's the thing, wherein we'll catch the conscience of the King.'

Good old Hamlet. The first scenes-of-crime reconstructor.

He was also careless enough to get himself killed in a rigged sword fight.

I passed through part of Glyntywyn and headed west on the main trunk road. The early-morning juggernaut traffic from the Irish ferries lumbered towards me. The sun was now well up. A cold day with clear blue sky above me. Fifteen miles away, in the direction of Llanmartin, the sky was clouding over.

The Experimental Weapons and Proof Testing Establishment occupied a plain eight miles long by two wide fronting on the flat, sandy Llanmartin bay. The base was equidistant from two villages. One was a regimented resort, with miles of caravans; the other, pretty and picturesque, with none. I turned off the minor road that had followed the base perimeter fence for over a mile. The main gates, set back several hundred yards from this road, were open.

I stopped the Cortina at the security barrier alongside the small gatehouse, glass-windowed on all sides for all round vision. Ministry of Defence Police notices sprouted everywhere. HALT, then ALL VISITORS REPORT TO GATEHOUSE, then SPEED LIMIT 5 MPH. The Ministry have the knack of making you feel welcome.

The old concrete roadway, the rusted chain-link perimeter fence and the tall grass growing wild on the flat land had the air of 1940s' movies — drab grey. Any moment I expected to hear old Vera Lynn records blaring over the tannoy and see the ghost of the indomitable Douglas Bader hobbling out to his Spitfire.

Instead, a stocky, blond M.O.D. Police character walked around my car, hands clasped behind his back, checking the registration of the Cortina. A youngster, practising the technique. From inside the gatehouse, a greying old stager kept a watchful eye on the proceedings.

"Yes, sir?" the youngster asked, giving the Cortina's interior the copper's once-over.

For this visit I was not Jeremy Hall. I was Halloran, carrying the Blue Security Pass. The youngster was puzzled at first. I doubted whether he had ever seen a Blue Pass before. There were only twenty-four in the country. I stepped out of the Cortina.

"Halloran. Fetch the duty S.O. for me, please."

This time the 'Yes, sir' was bracing, followed by a sharp salute.

The gatehouse smelled of tobacco and tea. Old-style black telephones stood to attention on a stained counter, alongside two intercoms. A kettle perched in a corner next to three mugs. The youngster was already on the phone to someone when the old stager wandered over, trying to appear disinterested. He had seen the Blue Pass all right. The grin on his long face was one of surprised insecurity. Self-consciously he lit a cigarette and then offered me one. I declined.

There was no point in being subtle. I had caught a whiff of guilt in the air. And not the kind that comes from being caught unawares.

"Base status?"

"Alpha Black, sir."

"Visiting Personnel Day Book."

There was something anticipatory in the old stager's attitude. For a Monday morning he found that Day Book much too quickly.

Everyone entering or leaving any top secret base on official business had to sign in and sign out, daily. That signature had to be countersigned by the gate officer-in-charge. Every week the Base Security Officer would sign it, confirming it as a true record. Omega Section were the only exceptions. We rarely signed anything, particularly expenses chits. I checked the book and the security personnel signatures were all in order. Between 11 January and 15 January inclusive Jack Lane's signature appeared twice daily. That tallied with the file. But on Tuesday and Wednesday the 14th and 15th Jack had not signed the book. The signatures looked like his. They would possibly have fooled a handwriting expert. But not me. The gate officer who had countersigned those forgeries was named Thomas.

"Who's Thomas?"

46

"Me, sir."

His hazel eyes never wavered. I lit a cigarillo and looked at the book again, then at Thomas. For a flickering millisecond those eyes looked away before staring back at me once more.

I had once been a damned good Army Officer. Not so hot on the etiquette, like the correct way to pass the port and staying away from the bored, nympho wives of more senior officers — my eventual undoing. But when I said 'Jump' or 'Follow me', everyone did. I had seen men drunk, petrified, sullen, sinful, proud, alive and dead. And I knew when someone was giving me a load of bullshit.

Thomas was trying to. Then my inbuilt survival mechanism took over. I had to keep my mouth shut. If there was a conspiracy, I needed to know how far it went. Anyway, no-one knew where I was. If I really had hit trouble they could bury me under a sand dune and no-one would be any the wiser.

Then a Land Rover pulled up alongside the gatehouse, giving me the excuse not to pursue the matter any further, for the moment.

Chapter 7

A BALD, ROUND-FACED man wearing gardening clothes emerged from the Land Rover. He glanced at my car in passing and shook my hand as soon as he came into the gatehouse.

"Hello there, I'm Barrett. Base S.O." The voice was West Country, the handshake firm.

"Halloran. Shall we go to your office?"

I followed the Land Rover in my car. The main base complex was a mile away, past sheds, bunkers, antennae and observation towers. A dog handler patrolled scrub to my left while to the right another Land Rover criss-crossed the area. Either their security status was A1 at all times or news of my arrival had spread quickly. I had asked for the duty S.O. but got the Chief who had obviously been digging the garden on his day off. They were either terrified at the sight of a Blue Pass or someone had a guilty conscience.

Barrett's office was lined with filing cabinets and furnished with his own desk and three uncomfortable chairs. A functional room, for working from, not loafing around in. He made coffee himself, the good stuff, not the usual Ministry sweepings off the warehouse floor complete with sawdust particles.

"What brings you?" Barrett asked, pleasantly.

"Curiosity."

"I just wondered how much trouble you can be," he joked.

"Short of nuclear war you'll never have more."

He realized I was not being humorous. The round face creased into a worrying-about-my-pension frown.

"I check the paperwork." I smiled.

He gave me the kind of look that said: 'If you check the paperwork, then I'm the Archbishop of Canterbury.'

"I've seen your Visiting Personnel Day Book. S.O.3 Jack Lane who inspected recently was on base eleventh to the fifteenth of January inclusive. Am I correct?"

The open face was now clouded with concern. I was building a mental picture of Barrett and hoped it was the correct one. Cool under awkward questioning, efficient, a little homespun, capable of inspiring loyalty in his subordinates. Not a by-the-book merchant but a get-the-job-done man. I had him worried.

"You heard Lane was dead?" I asked.

"Yes. I was sorry to hear that. I liked him. Here's a copy of the Base Status report he filed. Gave us an Alpha."

"Bully for you."

The Base Status report was the same one I had seen before in Verity's file. Jack had signed that all right but not on the 15th despite the fact that the form bore that date. Otherwise he would have signed the book at the gatehouse. Probable explanation: These clowns were covering for him. I flicked through the Base Status reports for the previous two years. Jack had done the last three inspections.

I didn't have time to enter into a lengthy discussion. I would have to expose Barrett's weakness, the base's weakness. So I called the gatehouse on Barrett's desk phone and said:

"Thomas. Get your arse up to the Base S.O. on the double. Bring the Visiting Personnel Day Book with you."

Then Barrett and I looked at each other. I had the measure of his weakness now. He wanted to protect his man. I guessed Thomas's weakness would be loyalty to his boss. Before Barrett could protest I told him:

"Wait outside when Thomas gets here, if you don't mind."

He did. But there wasn't much he could do about it. Exit Barrett and two minutes later enter Thomas smartly to attention. I was in Barrett's chair now and the psychology of it was not lost on Thomas. I invited him to sit. He told me he'd rather stand. Which was when I got cross.

"Sit down," I ordered, coldly.

He obeyed, silently furious, and probably ready to break my neck.

"Ex-warrant officer. Which regiment?"

"Welsh Guards, sir."

"Any action?"

"Cyprus and Borneo, sir."

"Good. I'll spell it out. Jack Lane was the world's sloppiest sod for paperwork. He forgot to sign out the last two days he was here. You helped him out. Correct?"

"That would be a serious breach of procedure. Dismissable offence."

"If I decide so, you're a security risk. That means you're out minus pension rights. Besides chronic unemployment, you'll have to contend with my reference. Not good."

"You can't do that."

"On my say-so, the Pope is a security risk. With him there'd be an enquiry. With you, forget it. Jack Lane wasn't on this base after Monday the thirteenth of January. Correct?"

"You'll have to ask the Base S.O., sir."

"I'm asking you."

Thomas could see a lifetime down the tubes. I had him in the Catch 22 of dismissal for breach of procedure or dismissal on my word. The hazel eyes never left mine as he said:

"Mr Lane asked me to do him a favour. I did, on my own authority. Mr Barrett was not consulted, sir."

"You're a liar. Barrett talked you into it. Get out. Make sure your resignation is on this desk by the end of your shift."

He stood up and for a split second I thought an attack was imminent. The eyes were watering. With an effort, he saluted. I had robbed him of the rest of his working life. And he wasn't going to let me off that easily.

"You're a bastard."

"That's why I hold the Blue Pass. Fetch Barrett."

Two minutes and thirty seconds later Barrett returned. He said heavily:

"I ordered Thomas to doctor those signatures."

The cheery expression had gone. In the space of half an hour I had destroyed two careers. He was asking himself why.

"You want to explain?"

"No, sir. I will now write my resignation. I have no further statement to make. Nor will I have."

Sod's Law again. I had been too hard. They thought I was a martinet. And no way would Barrett let a martinet force him to break his word to Jack Lane. Yes, he had covered for Jack to go and do something else.

"Barrett, I'm short of time. Jack gave you that Base Status Report before he left here Monday night, signed but undated. He asked you to cover for him, perhaps for a couple of days, but forgot to fiddle the Visitors' Book. He didn't get back to you so you called his hotel. They told you he had checked out Thursday morning. So, you put the date on the report and hey presto. Then he's found dead. You've been dreading an inspection in case an investigation was forthcoming. Correct?"

Barrett said nothing, but from his expression I knew I had hit the truth. The other possibility was that he was involved in Jack's death. The facts were capable of that more sinister interpretation. But Barrett and Thomas weren't conspirators, just reasonable men trying to do someone who had become a mate a favour. Jack had that effect on people.

"I don't buy that bullshit about him dying on that mountain.

Jack was an ace at the undercover game years back. I think he was playing it down here. Years back he would never have been sloppy enough not to make sure you covered his tracks better than you've done. Were I not such a perceptive, aggressive fellow I'd have left here believing that story. A belief which might have got me killed. I want whoever killed Jack and I'll bust you or Thomas or anyone else who gets in my way. Understand?"

Barrett did. He opened up. Point in his favour. Criminal guilt usually clams up when confronted.

"So you're a clever bastard, Halloran. I gave Jack Lane my word I'd cover for him. But now he's dead I don't suppose it matters. Can I have one of those cigarillos?"

I lit one for each of us. Barrett drew in deeply and began.

"I got to know Jack Lane well from previous visits here and I liked him. He told me his history. Now his past inspections had been no more than adequate but this time he was spot on. He had the bit between his teeth for some enquiry he was on which he said was personal. He was making enquiries about the death of this girl."

Barrett rummaged in the desk. His thick fingers came up with a photograph. Blonde girl, late teens or early twenties, wearing a two-piece swimsuit that just about covered everything, and there was plenty to cover. Holiday-type snapshot, no photographer's credit, taken on the deck of a cabin cruiser against a background of other boats in a marina somewhere. A pretty girl, suntanned and smiling. Now dead.

"Stick with it, Barrett."

"Her name was Madsen, Natasha Madsen, and she fell to her death from a balcony during a party at a house in Jenkin's Quay before Christmas. Jack had a newspaper cutting with him dated the seventh of January detailing an inquest report. Verdict was accidental death. He wanted background information from me on the house's owner, Garth Gwyn."

The second time I had heard that name.

"Tell me exactly what you told Jack. This is important."

"Garth Gwyn and his elder brother Alan are the two partners in a big business concern locally. They own pubs, construction and

51

civil engineering businesses in Glyntywyn, holiday property and a real money-spinner, a country club and casino called the Willows. That's out of town to the east. People come from all over South Wales and even the Midlands there. The inevitable stories go round that this area is their personal fiefdom, that they influence the local authorities, entertain the right people and enjoy police co-operation because the local super is married into the family. Maybe it's gossip but I wouldn't trust Alan Gwyn as far as I could throw his casino, and I don't know him at all well. And I won't have any of my people going there."

"Why not?"

"You can lose money gambling. That lifestyle and this work don't mix. Nothing has ever happened as far as I know. But it pays to be cautious."

"So the Gwyns would be capable of dodgy dealings. Like faking the real cause of a death, and they could get police help?"

Barrett considered his reply very carefully.

"Possibly."

"When did you last see Jack?"

"Monday the thirteenth at six-thirty when he left here. He told me he was going to the Willows that night. But he did call me early Tuesday morning, about seven. He wanted to know if I'd heard of an American called Bill Ives who worked at the U.S. Naval Facility at Whitesands Head along the coast."

"Had you?"

"No. He said he'd cracked the problem, though."

"This American base. What happens there?"

"Tracking station for submarines. They have a computer there and it may be a control centre for watching the Western Approaches in conjunction with NATO. We have nothing to do with them."

"And I'm the only other person you've told?"

We looked each other straight in the eye and I knew he was telling me the truth. I had one last question.

"Was Jack carrying?"

"Yes. I didn't think Five did on inspections. Browning automatic."

I left Barrett with some good advice. If I called him and asked for the moon he should provide it. If anyone else called him, he had never seen me. Which would save us all the embarrassment of publicizing our little secrets and breaches of procedure. On my way out, I stopped at the gatehouse. Thomas emerged. He looked as if he would cheerfully shoot me.

"Thomas, I was never here."

"No, sir." He looked puzzled now.

"Because if I was, I'd have to file a report. And I'd hate for it to get round that you called me a bastard and lived to collect your pension."

I parked the Cortina in Glyntywyn and ambled around the town. Money there, all right. Five banks and numerous building societies to put it in. Three supermarkets, five jewellers, eight shoe-, twelve clothes-, five multiple- and numerous other shops to spend it in. Seven estate agents would find you somewhere to live while you spent it and ten solicitors would plunder it when you had gone. But only three accountants would advise you how to invest it. They must have had an endless lunch round with the building society managers.

The office blocks were mostly clustered away from the shops and newly built. The tax, the V.A.T., and the D.H.S.S. rubbed shoulders with the Ministry of Agriculture, the Water quango and the Development quango. All the bureaucrats in close proximity. Maybe they reproduced better that way.

Across another car park, the Council and the Police had superb accommodation in expensive, architect-designed blocks overlooking the river. Money all right and the bureaucrats were first in line for the luxurious working amenities. All the new building I could see was contracted by the Gwyn brothers and they always used the same firm of architects. Probably had shares in that.

I meandered into a small papershop. The notice in the window stated it was soon due to close. The terrace in which it was situated was scheduled for redevelopment, presumably into more offices. I spoke Welsh to the obliging shrivelled old lady. She found me the January 7th issue of the local paper from a pile of firelighters in the

53

upstairs living quarters while I watched the shop for her. I spoke Welsh for two reasons. One, she was more likely to help a fellow native. Two, she was almost certain not to recall me as a stranger.

The Swan's lounge bar had been very recently redecorated. I could still smell the paint. Maybe that was why the place was mostly empty, because the beer was drinkable and the prices as reasonable as anywhere. I dawdled over a couple of pints which saw me over a very quiet lunchtime session. I know something about the licensed trade. I spend a lot of time in pubs and I keep my eyes open. That pub should have been busy. It had all the bar snack menus and the rolls and sandwiches in place. But it wasn't. Then I heard some general gossip from one end of the bar, between an old farmer and a short, mild-mannered character whose heavy face was topped with thinning grey hair. Obviously the landlord, Frank's mate, Bill Islwyn Evans, he wore a worried expression when he told how a major brawl had started in that same lounge midway through an evening session the previous Wednesday. The police had taken half an hour to get there, by which time the place had been wrecked. I thought that strange because the cops could have walked it in less than five minutes from their luxurious offices.

We started talking some minutes later. I was playing the weary traveller with nothing better to do than drink whisky. It soon became apparent that he was not going to talk about the local police or the local controlling interest named Gwyn. Whenever I raised the subjects he skirted round them and his eyes constantly flickered around the room, watching anyone who might be in a position to hear our conversation. He was scared of something or someone. When I mentioned that Frank told me Jack Lane had been in the area recently I thought mine host was suffering from cardiac failure.

He said no more and vanished into the public bar from where he cast occasional surreptitious glances in my direction. Someone had obviously warned him off mentioning Jack Lane. I wondered whether that had anything to do with half his pub being wrecked by the local yobbery.

I was making him feel uncomfortable and running the risk of being noticed. So I left Islwyn Evans to his fears and took up my reservation at the Lion Hotel in time for afternoon tea which I didn't want. Modern, overlooking the river, it had the chain-store brand of décor, bench leather and uniformed receptionists. I made sure they all saw my briefcase and pitch book, the salesman's bible. Good cover requires the tools of the particular trade you're pretending to ply.

A porter took my luggage to a spacious room overlooking the river. I asked him where the action was in this town, wink, wink and he knew. Go to the Willows. Adamson, the Lion's manager, would fix temporary membership. I gave him a fiver and waited two minutes after he closed the door. Then I checked the room for wiring. Paranoia to you maybe, second nature to old Halloran. The room was clean. I put all the paperwork I didn't want anyone to see into a large manila envelope and addressed it to myself at the cover address used by Omega Section. Then I went to look for the back way out of the hotel. As I walked back from the post office I had this feeling about Glyntywyn. Short-sighted policemen and powerful controlling interests were always bad news. Back in my room I reread the newspaper report about the inquest on Natasha Madsen.

Brief and to the point. She was a holidaying Swiss national who fell off the balcony of Garth Gwyn's house at Jenkin's Quay during a very late-night party on 19 December. The house overlooked the bay. It had been built on the clifftop for that purpose. Doubtless the architect had not envisaged girls full of LSD tumbling the one hundred and fifty feet to the rocky shore below. The Coroner's jury had paid particular attention to the police report which stated that although the girl had taken drugs, there was no evidence to suggest they had been available to the other party guests. Two witnesses stated they were positive no drugs were circulating at the party. One was a man named Kelly, described as a business consultant, the other a student named Stuart Jacobs. Superintendent J. C. Daniels had given evidence on the police report. Summing up, the Coroner said he had every sympathy for Mr Garth Gwyn who must have found the stigma of being thought to entertain junkies a very distressing experience.

So, Jack Lane. Where the hell did you go from here? And what sort of a front did you put up at this very hotel?

Chapter 8

AT SEVEN O' CLOCK that same Monday night I went for a drink. The Residents' Bar of the Lion looked like a good place to start asking discreet questions. They would remember Jack being in there.

The local brew was high octane stuff and the girl dispensing it seemed like she could be: big blue eyes, dark hair cut short and an unmethodist smile. When she crossed the room I saw the rest of her: legs that went all the way up, hips that swayed, and a narrow waist. Years back, Jack Lane's type of girl. So he would have made a few complimentary, if suggestive, remarks. And everyone remembered Jack's opening lines, if only because they were so bloody predictable.

I started with the line about my liking the Lion and the next time I saw my regular golfing chum Jack Lane I'd thank him for his recommendation. She was surprised I hadn't heard. I asked about what. She replied he had been for a walk on the mountains and got caught in the snow, permanently. She was just telling me about how dangerous the hills actually were in winter when we were interrupted. A tall, ramrod-straight young man wearing a pale if curious expression, homed in like a heat-seeking missile at the mention of Jack's name.

"I'm Adamson, the manager," he introduced himself.

There was no need. The morning suit and the gold-framed glasses spelled out hotelier.

"Did you know Mr Lane well?" he asked.

"He recommended good hotels to me during our infrequent rounds of golf."

"Sad business," he commiserated, then changed the subject: "You asked at Reception for membership at the Willows. All fixed for whenever you like."

He moved off, but I noticed him come through the bar twice more during the next ten minutes. Each time he looked to see if I was still talking to the girl. She told me her name was Susan. I told her mine was Jeremy and felt ridiculous. I didn't even like the name Jeremy.

"Mr Adamson doesn't like us talking about Mr Lane," she confided. "He says it's bad publicity for the hotel."

"Dead people must have stayed somewhere," I replied.

She thought that was funny and changed the subject. But I did manage to persuade her to have a drink with me somewhere else when she came off duty. She agreed, reluctantly, knowing that I wanted to hear more, but asked me to go on ahead. She wasn't keen on Adamson seeing us together.

Susan was one minute late arriving in the Hart, a quiet hostelry far enough away from the Lion for her to feel comfortable. Yet she kept looking around the lounge bar to see if she knew anyone there. She smoked her cigarette too quickly and drummed her fingers nervously on the table. Deep in her eyes I read concern, for what she was about to tell me and its possible consequences.

"Why are you so interested?" she asked.

"Curious, that's all."

She looked coldly at me. I had said the wrong thing. Susan was a bright girl and I would have to be more honest with her if I wanted the truth. I offered her money and her eyes blazed angrily. Teach you to be cynical, Halloran. So I came as clean as I could.

"Jack was a very old friend. His girlfriend didn't buy the story of how he died. When she heard I was coming to the area, she asked me to look around. I'm just doing what I can."

"Mr Lane was in the bar Saturday night. He was asking questions about Alan Gwyn and his brother Garth, about the sort of people they were. He was out a lot while he was here. Will you promise you won't tell anyone what I'm going to tell you?"

"Sure."

"Just before I left the hotel tonight, Mr Adamson warned me not to go alarming the guests. He meant it. Hints were dropped about sacking me. I need my job, Mr Hall. I have a daughter to support and I also have to live in this town. It doesn't pay to ask too many questions about the Gwyns. You take that from me. Now, Mr Lane went to the Willows on the Monday night and returned late with Mrs Elizabeth Gwyn, Alan's wife. She was seen leaving the hotel at seven the following morning. The Gwyns own the Lion, remember."

Inference clear, Jack indulging in adultery with the controlling interest. Not like Jack, to go for a casual one-night stand when operational unless he had a very good reason.

"After they found the body the police came around. I am sure Mr Lane left the hotel on the Tuesday morning. I told a policeman so. Mr Adamson said I was mistaken, it was Thursday because he had seen Mr Lane himself. He even produced the booking cards. Mr Lane's was written out in Adamson's own writing. Not very often does he write out booking cards, I can tell you."

"I don't suppose you'd give me a written statement to that effect?" I asked.

She shook her head. Now she was frightened. Without saying another word she looked betrayed and walked out of the door.

So far I had traced Jack Lane's movements up to seven am, Tuesday 14 January. According to Barrett, Jack had been carrying his Browning and was alive at that time. He had called Barrett after spending the night with Elizabeth Gwyn, who might have given Jack the reason for wanting to know more about this Bill Ives. Susan's statement meant that Adamson lied and Jack had left the Lion on the Tuesday morning. Yet the police report stated forty-eight hours later.

The obvious step was to locate and talk with Elizabeth Gwyn. I looked her husband's number up in the phone book and telephoned. An au pair answered. The Gwyns were at the Willows.

I took a taxi. Driving myself in an area where I didn't trust the police was asking for trouble. The Willows was fifteen miles out of Glyntywyn. Impressively floodlit from the outside, the nineteenth-century mansion had architect-designed extensions to gladden the planners' eyes. Inside, the facilities were varied, squash, swimming and other indoor sports, bars, restaurant and cabaret. And for the punters, fruit machines and a purpose-built gaming room with roulette, blackjack and chemin de fer.

I had worn my eagerly optimistic face at the door. Free from Charlotte, the kids and Biggles I was out to enjoy myself. I gave my false name and clumsily knocked the membership book on the floor. By the time I had put it back and signed it, I knew Jack Lane's signature was missing. So was an entire page for Monday 13 January. It must have been their unlucky night. Business must have been bad, judging by the shortage of signatures.

Not like tonight, which seemed lively enough. Not interested in the yokels, the Willows catered for the expense account brigade, and the people with real money to spend. I wandered around for a while, getting the feel of the place. The new industrialists were there, with their micro-chip technology from the grant-aided development areas that were their meal ticket to Euro-markets. Easily accessible from the valleys, Swansea or even the Midlands, the Willows was taking the city money and even some of the oil loot from the west.

A helpful barman pointed the Gwyns out to me. They were among a small group of the middle class, middle Welsh, the Mercedes owners with their gin and tonic manners, Cardiff Arms Park debentures and villas on the Algarve.

Alan Gwyn was one of life's natural hosts, conspicuously ordering large ones in a deep, authoritative voice. Flamboyant, red-haired and heavy-faced, he had deep-set hazel eyes that noticed everything. A big man. Not tall but powerful. One to watch out for. A man who wanted to be seen as successful. I doubted whether he'd take kindly to my waltzing over and asking if I could just have a word with his wife about a recent affair of hers.

Elizabeth Gwyn was fifteen years younger than her husband. Early thirties. The flaming red hair, tall, statuesque physique and the style of her pale-yellow evening dress marked her as someone special. A fiery Celt. I could see why Jack had noticed her. She had the same hard good looks as his ex-wife. Knowing Jack's luck, she probably had the same predatory temperament.

I wondered how these surface people had been involved in Jack's death. He was a pro. Maybe a pro who had skidded off the

59

rails, but not that far. These people were successful, affluent, but not that smart. Surely not? Small-time businessmen made good local corrupters, the sort to bribe local councillors and perhaps bully appointed officials, maybe with the help of a few yokel cops. But outmanoeuvre old Jack?

When Elizabeth Gwyn left the bar, I followed. A couple of passing women gave me strange looks as I hung around outside the Ladies Room. When Elizabeth Gwyn emerged, I stood in her way.

"Hello, I'm being discreet. I'd like to talk with you about Jack Lane."

She looked me up and down, trying to pretend I was some kind of nut. A good act, it gave her time for some fast thinking. Her pale-green eyes would not look straight at me.

"I'm sorry. You must have the wrong person."

Her voice was hard, insistent.

"No mistake," I reassured her. "Shall we discuss it with your husband?"

I blame it on the easier divorce laws. Even fifteen years ago when I started in the game, an insinuation like that would have been enough to bring a recalcitrant informer to her senses. Not now. She pushed past me and went looking for her husband.

From the look he gave me when he thought I wasn't watching, she must have told him about our brief encounter. I jammed my back against the corner of the bar in case he sent some of the house muscle to eject me. But no. Half an hour later, the group moved off and I was left contemplating my ginger ale. Never drink too much when working. After twenty more minutes and another ginger ale I was ready to look for her again when she appeared beside me. Chanel perfume mingled with the aroma of her Black Russian cigarette.

"I was very rude," she apologized. The accent was muted but it was still a hard accent, east of Cardiff hard.

"Drink?" I asked.

"Gin and tonic. Thank you for being sensible."

Not the adjective I'd have used. It had the overtones of: Be a sensible man or you'll get your skull crushed.

Her green eyes flickered in the direction of the barman and she moved to a vacant corner table. I followed.

"You're not local," she said quietly. "Where are you staying?"

"Lion."

"We'll go there in a minute. I don't want to talk here."

She finished her drink with practised speed. She wasn't drunk but she shouldn't have been driving. We went out the back way to the darkened part of the car park and I suspected a trap. My stomach tightened in expectation of being jumped by big, heavy men. The sort who break your brittle bones and laugh. I kept watching the shadows while she unlocked a Mercedes 230 sports car.

No-one jumped me. But the worst moments were to come. She drove like a determined suicide case. Headlights weaved crazy patterns along narrow lanes where the road and my stomach dropped away in several places. She wouldn't talk and I didn't encourage her. She needed all her concentration for the road. Against the odds we made it into Glyntywyn where she slowed down to a steady fifty. Instead of parking in the Lion car park she left the Mercedes a street away. She took my arm and as we walked she said:

"My husband doesn't approve of my nocturnal expeditions."

"Where is he now?"

"Entertaining for the next few hours. Don't worry."

She'd had practice in this game. She even knew the back way into the hotel. And no-one saw us enter my room.

"Did you spend a night in this hotel with Jack Lane?"

"Yes."

"So what happened to him afterwards?"

"Just who are you?"

"Jeremy Hall, an old friend of his."

"Well, Jeremy Hall, do you think you could find me some Scotch? Then we'll talk about your friend. I liked him."

The inference was clear. If she liked me, I was in for the same exhibition Jack got. I couldn't make up my mind whether she was drunk, play-acting or slightly insane. One thing I did detect was a nervous insecurity bordering on fear. I can smell fear at thirty paces.

61

Room service arrived with the Scotch. The porter poured me a glass while Elizabeth Gwyn hid in the bathroom. As the door closed she emerged on tiptoe clutching a tumbler.

"You've done this before. What if your husband finds out?"

She looked serious for a moment then shook her head.

"He won't."

"Jack was asking questions. What did he want to know?"

"Who was at the party the night Natasha fell from the balcony."

"Who was?"

She fiddled with her whisky glass. I took a good slug at mine.

"I was. Garth was. So was Bill Ives. But Bill told us not to let on to anyone else that he'd been there. We obliged. John Daniels got a bit huffy about it all but he doesn't like Bill. Bill knows too much."

"About what?"

She stood up for a moment and smiled at me.

"Do you think I'm beautiful?"

"Exquisitely so," I replied. You shouldn't really tell lies but it wasn't really a lie. Personality a bit off but Elizabeth had a lot going for her in other ways.

"What does Bill know too much about?" I asked.

She clammed up on me then. I stood up and walked over to her. Halfway across the room my legs gave out on me. I could hear her voice saying "I'm sorry. I'm sorry", but it was far away.

I was tumbling through a mental vortex. I had this vision of Alan Gwyn laughing at me while Elizabeth lolled on the bed and said "I'm sorry". The last coherent thought I had was that I'd been too slow, too clumsy and had underrated the opposition. Then as the black oblivion engulfed me I heard the whisky glass hitting the floor.

Chapter 9

I WAS AWARE of a dim light. It could have been my brain re-activating or something outside my field of slowly-returning vision. The ceiling eventually stopped circling like a kaleidoscope but I had to make a real effort to keep my eyes open.

No windows, no loose fixtures of any kind. Off-white walls in an enclosed room. The smell of whisky, a lot of whisky. Police cell. It had to be. Footsteps sounded in a concrete corridor. I tried to get up and failed. An eye appeared at the peephole in the heavy metal door. The door opened with the magnified sound of a thousand rusty hinges. I focused my eyes on an expanse of light-blue stomach. Somewhere a voice said:

"Slept it off at last? Christ, you smell like a brewery. On your feet."

They did not stand on ceremony in this nick. I was hauled to a pair of wobbly things that might have been my legs. They didn't give me the chance to find out. A light-blue mass at each side of me seized my arms. Big boys. They probably propped for the local Police XV. I tried to walk up the steps but my escorts were impatient. They dragged me instead.

Interrogation room. Table, two fixed benches and a rubberoid concrete floor. The door slammed shut. I felt dizzy and sick. I was sick, in the adjacent doorless toilet. It smelled like booze. It had the bitter taste of booze but I hadn't drunk that much.

They had used something on me, whoever they were. Some kind of tranquillizer. My mind tried to focus. Where had I been? What the hell had happened? No good. The mental pictures were a fuzzy, multi-coloured mess. Eventually I realized I was standing up, dressed in shirt, trousers, underwear, socks and no shoes. Concentrate Halloran. Fix the mind on something and take it from there. I chose a mark on the back of the locked steel door.

63

Continual footsteps sounded outside the room. Doors banged, voices mumbled, someone was whistling. Interrogation room. Resistance to interrogation. I had not dodged that course. Establish cover. Think cover. Cover. I am Halloran, Omega. No. No. I am Jeremy Hall, aged thirty-eight, and the boys that know call me the Headhunter. Stop. Your mind's wandering. Concentrate. I am Jeremy Hall, married with two children and Biggles. Ah, Biggles, you lovely fat Labrador. Better. Better. Wife's name? Wife's name? Christ, man, you must know your wife's name. Charlotte. That's it. The lovely Charlotte. Last night, I went to the Willows. I met Elizabeth Gwyn. I asked her about Jack Lane. No. No. Steady, Jeremy Hall. Maybe that's the part you're not supposed to remember. Mrs Gwyn, the hard redhead who wanted Scotch . . .

The steel door opened. Either they had recently oiled the hinges or my brain was rejoining the rest of my head. Two men entered heavily. I braced myself for the attack. But no. Not yet, anyway. These boys were carrying paperwork.

The first was young, boy-faced, with a moustache to hide his youth and wide brown eyes to confirm it. Lean and tall, his hands were thrust deep into trouser pockets.

His mate was thick-set, bull-necked and older. The square face was heavy-boned and the blue eyes unfriendly. His voice was deep, booming, authoritative.

"Tea," he announced as a uniformed man set a tray down on the table.

I needed something to drink. My throat felt thick and clogged up. Wait. Think clearly. Something to drink landed you in here. I remembered the whisky in the hotel room. Elizabeth Gwyn had asked for whisky. She drank gin at the Willows.

"No thanks." My voice was not my own. It belonged to some furry alcoholic with iron filings in his larynx.

Bullneck shrugged and stirred his tea. The noise rattled around my head.

"What happened?" I asked. Drunkard's question but it might give me some idea of the game they were playing. They both thought that was funny. Neither laugh was friendly. Then they started the old two to one routine beloved of yokel cops the world over. Brown Eyes stopped laughing and said:

"So you don't remember drinking at the Willows, then at your hotel? I suppose you've forgotten all about wrecking your room and getting nasty with a lady when she said No?"

So that was the story. Jeremy, you walked right into that. Your alter ego, Halloran, underestimated the opposition. Now, Jeremy, you must play this in character. You're an educated man and you know your rights.

"What time is it?"

"Answer the question." Bullneck was losing his cool.

"I want a solicitor."

"When I'm ready." Bullneck grinned smugly at Brown Eyes.

"There must be some mistake. I'm lovable when I'm drunk, not aggressive."

Brown Eyes repeated the words, then wrote them down. Selective verbals. So that was the style in this nick.

"Sales executive, I understand," Brown Eyes continued. "I wonder what your employer would say about you smashing up hotel rooms and assaulting women."

There was a severe strain of righteous Methodism in his voice.

"I didn't smash anything or anyone."

Bullneck's heavy fist landed on the table. The message was simple but effective. Next time it would be my ribs. He spoke loudly and sounded threatening. Not difficult for him.

"We have received two complaints. Malicious damage from the manager of the Lion Hotel and a far more serious one from Mrs Elizabeth Gwyn. You assaulted her in your hotel room. Some kind of pervert, are you? Get your kicks from clouting women? I don't like perverts."

"They're lying," I replied.

Brown Eyes restrained Bullneck's righteous fist that would have smashed my head on the table.

"We've got evidence," Brown Eyes said coldly.

If that was the case, why hadn't they already charged me? In this nick, they had never heard of the Judges' Rules. No caution. Then the wrong form of words denying me access to a solicitor. So they wanted a confession. No way.

"You'll lose your bloody job," Bullneck promised. "Watch him close. I'll be back. Bloody fool, he's still pissed."

Alone with Brown Eyes now. He lit a cigarette, did not offer me one and whispered:

"Mrs Gwyn said you were asking about a man named Lane when you assaulted her."

"I can't remember. But I doubt it."

He did not have time to elaborate before Bullneck returned carrying a pack of cigarettes. He didn't offer me one either. But the message had got through.

"Book him," Bullneck ordered.

The silence was well-timed. But they left it too long before continuing the charade. Brown Eyes whispered to Bullneck:

"Bad publicity for everyone concerned. Wouldn't Gwyn consider a deal?"

He spoke loudly enough for me to hear. Then they decided it was time to confer amongst themselves, outside.

A long time passed. They were sweating me. And I was supposed to act nervous, to consider my position. Time for Jeremy Hall to act in character, to act penitent. Think of Justin and Samantha and old Biggles. Think of poor Charlotte. She'd never be able to hold up her head in the Church Drama Group again. Think of your career, Jeremy Hall. More to the point, think of your career, Halloran. If this cover doesn't hold they might cover you — permanently.

I paced up and down for a long time. I acted scared. That part wasn't too difficult, considering what had happened to Jack. Eventually Brown Eyes came back.

"Sit down, Mr Hall, and listen. My sergeant is a right bastard."

You can say that again, I thought.

"All I want to do is save the paperwork. I've spoken to Mr Gwyn. His wife is naturally very upset. It's going to be very embarrassing for her to make a court appearance if you plead not guilty. Now he might be prepared to withdraw the complaint."

I looked suitably eager.

"If you leave Glyntywyn and never, ever come back. I think I can swing it."

"What do I tell my firm?" I asked, innocently.

"That's your problem. What would you prefer, explaining to your boss or having my sergeant persuading you to plead guilty?"

The expression on his face told me that could be a very painful option.

"Think about it," he invited.

I did, for a long time. They left me alone again. I really had lost track of time. There was nothing to relate to, nothing to fiddle with. Standard police procedure. A subtle form of disorientation. I acted nervous again for so long I almost was nervous.

The door opened again. Bullneck marched back in. He pushed me towards a corner.

"My milk of human kindness colleague has persuaded Mr Gwyn it would be better if he never saw you again."

I knew the punch was coming. You always do. I tensed my stomach muscles again. The short, powerful jab doubled me up and I fell. My stomach was in my mouth, not for the first time today.

"You ever come back to this town and I'll kick you to pieces," Bullneck warned.

I lay there gasping for a while. Then I staggered to my feet and promised myself a return bout with that ugly thick excrescence. Ten minutes later Brown Eyes came back with my possessions which I checked against the property list he handed me. Then I signed it. No-one else had. Another mistake, boys. But Jeremy Hall wouldn't know that. I counted the money in my wallet. There had been over sixty quid in it last night. Only twenty came back. Cheeky bastards. So that was how they topped up the station beer fund. Everything else was there, except the newspaper cutting I had taken from the local rag concerning the inquest on Natasha Madsen. Careless of me. But I let it go. All I wanted to do was get out of there.

Brown Eyes insisted on calling me a taxi. I told the driver to take me to the Lion. I wound the back window down to give me some fresh air and that was a mistake. I felt dizzy again. My throat was still like the Gobi desert and I really did need a drink. It was dark outside, whether morning or night I didn't know. Then I remembered something else they had taken from me in the nick. My temporary membership card for the Willows. Now that was . . .

I really was having a very slow day. Before I even knew it had happened, the taxi had stopped, near the river, and two big shapes loomed at each open rear door of the taxi. A gun barrel was jammed into my ribs and I was dragged out. A blow to the base of my neck stunned me but I was still conscious. The taxi had gone and a door had closed. The first boot hit me in the kidneys and I fell face down on to an oily concrete floor.

I was in no fit state to fight my way through a wet newspaper. No way could I take both of them in my weakened condition. I tasted oil and sawdust, felt as though half my body was missing, and with a supreme effort I rolled away. But you never, ever give up. As the next boot came in I caught it with both hands and twisted, hard. Its owner yelped and spun in mid-air. But I was too late to stop a boot in the groin from the second man. Through blurred, double, painful vision I could see a heavy face with cold blue eyes. My friend Bullneck. Then my head was snapped sideways, my eyeballs jarred and I was down again. A wet, sticky sensation on my spinning head, another boot in the kidneys and I was fighting for non-existent air. A rushing sound filled my ears.

Somewhere in the distance, I could hear a heavy, monotonous voice laughing. I tried to open my eyes but something had closed them up for me. More kicks. I threw up. The world fell through a crazy vortex of pain to black, endless despair. Silence. A gun. I had seen a gun. Hang on to it, Halloran. An image of a gun.

"You're a hard man, Halloran," I kept telling myself. "Drugged, half-dead, a shapeless man of pain, but you can do it. You're the Headhunter. So, go on. Get up."

Over and over again I told myself to get up. I could get up. I would get up. I would walk back to the hotel, collect my car, phone Frank to bring the Magnum and go looking for those two apes. I would do a clog dance on Bullneck's heavy, blue-eyed face. Set me up for a kicking, would he? I would teach him to come and join in.

Then I would locate Elizabeth and screw the truth out of her, if necessary. After that I would take the Willows apart, Gwyns and all, and then have a few words with that brown-eyed copper about the finer points of the Judges' Rules. No-one beat the Headhunter mostly dead and got away with it. They might have done Jack Lane, but not Halloran.

I only had one small problem. Getting up off that oily, sawdust-strewn floor. I willed myself on with thoughts of vengeance because hate was the only thing stronger than the unbearable pain that racked my entire body. I could do it. My feet worked and I could lift my legs. So there was no permanent damage to my spine. Hell, I was on my feet now and my legs worked, just. Only my imagination told me I had gone fifteen rounds with a Chieftain tank. I half saw, half touched my way through a door and stumbled into a washroom. It was filthy, and the sink was rust-stained and grimy. But the taps worked. I propped myself against the basin, anchored myself against the opposite wall by stretching one leg, and turned the water full on. The cold, breathtaking torrent ran over my head, down my neck and back, soaking my shirt. My head was swollen where the pistol barrel had caught me. The blood had dried to a tacky mess which I swilled out of my hair along with the oil and bits of sawdust.

I was coming back to full consciousness. My senses were sharpening but so was the pain. I gulped water until my stomach was bloated and aching. Mistake. Natural reaction but a mistake. I felt my way along the wall and found a light switch. The lights worked. I was in an old workshop. My stomach turned over and I made the washroom before I threw up. At least I was sluicing whatever muck was still left in my offended system away, however painfully.

It was time to walk up and down. Nothing too ambitious, just gently exercise my legs. Left, right. Left, right. Better. My co-ordination was returning. Left, right. Left, right. I picked up my jacket. Left, right, left, right. Quicker now. Every movement hurt. My ribs ached. No, not more broken ribs. I was establishing a rhythm now. Left, right, left right. Pick up your feet, you 'orrible little man. Left, right, left right.

It was regulation march, and it took me half an hour before I was fit to even think about walking outside. The car keys were not in my jacket pocket. They had been when I left the nick. So I turned out the lights and opened an outside door very slowly. Darkness outside, with moonlit rain glistening on concrete. A stationary Cortina was parked outside. Very thoughtful of someone, considering it was my car.

I waited against the wall, allowing my eyesight to adjust to the darkness. Occasional traffic passed on the trunk road, a few hundred yards away. The rain was heavier now. Cold and wet though I was, that rain was better than the warmest sun. The pain eased and my reflexes sharpened up.

I had mentioned Jack Lane's name to Mrs Gwyn. Brown Eyes had used Jack's name. Brown Eyes and Bullneck set me up for a kicking from Bullneck and A. N. Other. Yet they wanted me out of town. That did not follow. If I suspected a cover-up, why let me go? The pointers were there for me to leave. A going-over after a deal where I was not supposed to come back. My car conveniently left for me. It didn't make sense.

I was about to open the car door when the ghost of Jack Lane started talking again. They could have killed you, H. So why didn't they? Why do they want you to leave? Remember, H, if the bastards want you to make a move, they set up all the pointers to encourage you to make it.

I lay down on the wet concrete and slid myself under the car. My matches were damp but the concrete beneath the car was dry. I managed to strike a match. There were no unauthorized attachments underneath the Cortina. I stood up again, opened the driver's door very carefully and found a small car torch. No-one had tampered with the ignition wiring inside. Now for the bonnet. I opened that very carefully. My stomach was knotted up again and the palms of my hands were sweating. The bonnet opened, I searched by torchlight.

And there it was, about the size of a paperback book, a metal container attached to the engine block. No extraneous wires. Which was strange. Most car bombers wired a detonator up to the ignition switch, using current to activate the bomb.

Suddenly I forgot the pain. Some literary genius once said that if you are facing the firing squad in the morning that fact enables you to concentrate the mind wonderfully. True. Very true. Because I started thinking hard and fast. The explosives course was one I had not dodged. Years ago maybe, but the brain is a tremendous piece of machinery. It remembers things you know you have forgotten, and very often just in time. Now. Why the engine block? Because engines heated up, didn't they? So the bomb was meant to explode after the engine had run for some time. Therefore, Halloran and Cortina not meant to go bang until some distance from Glyntywyn. Clever, Mr Bomber, whoever you are.

Detonator would therefore be activated by some kind of temperature rise. Hence the metal container which was taped on. Using my sharp penknife I cut the tape. My hands perspired as I worried about some kind of anti-handling device, maybe trembler activated. No. Not possible. Engine vibration would shake the container immediately. Therefore not a trembler device.

The metal container was heavy, or maybe it just seemed that way. The lid was the biscuit tin variety. I took a deep breath and started to ease the lid off. Stop. Stop. It could be a timing device in there, not detonated by heat at all but by some timing mechanism. So, the anti-handling device would be rigged to explode if the lid was taken off.

I put the container on the ground and looked at it for a moment. No point in calculating the odds on which type of detonator. Heat activated or timing. A bookmaker would give evens. But bombs told you a lot about who rigged them. I wanted to know what type of mind I was dealing with.

The choice was simple. Risk taking that lid off and possibly go up in smoke, or chuck the thing in the river and find some other way to discover the mind behind this little game. No contest. I chucked the thing in the river.

My suitcase was in the boot of the car. I chucked that in the river too. The best killers allow themselves more than one chance. Now all I had to do was drive myself away.

The seatbelt held me in the driving position. All of me hurt but I got under way somehow. The drive was agonizing. Headlights coming the opposite way danced painfully in my brain. My eyes were screwed up into slits and my hands were clamped damply on the steering wheel. For once I wished I was driving an automatic because every gear change was a new experience in pain.

It took me three hours to get there but I made it to Brecon just as dawn was breaking. I hammered on the door of the Blue Bell. Eventually a bleary-eyed Frank opened up.

"Jesus Christ," he exclaimed.

For a dozy old man Frank moved very quickly. He caught me as I fell.

Chapter 10

AN HOUR LATER I was eating scrambled eggs and drinking hot tea. Ten am Wednesday 29 January. So I had lost almost thirty-six hours being doped, gaoled and beaten up.

"You really ought to see a doctor," Frank insisted.

Correction, Frank. I needed a psychiatrist. Only a man who is insanely over-confident underestimates his opposition and walks knowingly into a trap. I had been lucky they decided to kill me by remote control and not take the safer course of a close-range pistol shot to the back of the head while I was unconscious in that warehouse.

I rushed for the toilet. The drugs had given me a severe dose of gastro-enteritis. I was weaker than Moshe Dayan's proverbial offspring.

Later on, Frank drove me to Cardiff and put me on the Inter-City for Paddington. The Cortina stayed in Frank's car park. I was too tired even to think straight. I slept on the train.

Moshe Dayan was waiting to greet me at 5.45 pm. He turned up his nose at the cat food I had bought him on the way from the station. The look he gave me said: "I like prawns." Ungrateful cat.

I opened the manila envelope I had posted myself from Glyntywyn and took out the Blue Pass. I had the nasty feeling that being without that might have saved my life. I put it on the bedside table, next to the Magnum. Jeremy Hall no longer existed. Halloran was going in next time around and he would find out the truth. But first he needed to recover, and quickly.

The hot bath helped soak away the already-stiffening agony. When the water cooled, I emptied the bath and repeated the process. Miraculously, my ribs were not broken this time.

At 10.15 pm I called Lucinda Bellamy, told her I was out of town but would have some information for her within forty-eight hours. That was all I told her. Then I took another bath and crawled into bed.

I woke at 5.21 am and made coffee. Verity's phone number had been among Jack Lane's possessions so it was a safe bet Verity had sent him unofficial, presumably to look into Natasha Madsen's death. I could not very well call Verity and ask him who Natasha Madsen was without giving the game away. I did know she was a Swiss national. So I called Gunther instead.

There was some difficulty about Swiss co-operation, for two reasons. One: Gunther did not appreciate being woken up early. Two: the bureaucratic adventurers from the Revenue had been at it again. Two investigators, trying to trace unpaid tax to a Zurich bank, had been clumsy. They had approached a bank official with a view to inspecting some books, purely out of academic interest, of course. But they had read their man wrongly. Swiss law compels a banker to respect more confidences than a priest. So the Criminal Police had bounced the fearless taxmen, handcuffed them and put them on the next London plane with the words: 'Persona non grata', the diplomatic euphemism for: 'Try that again and it's ten years digging fallout shelters under the Alps.'

All very humorous except the Swiss don't have a sense of humour, especially where financial confidentiality is concerned. Channels of co-operation had been closed temporarily. Which made life complicated for those of us with a real job of work to do. So I mortaged all my future goodwill and called in every past favour owing. Gunther promised to get back to me.

By 6.15 am I was in the Alamo. They were closing up after another profitable night. Sean's massive figure loomed up behind me.

"Christ, H, whose house hit you?"

I smiled and put on the dark glasses.

"One I'll demolish very soon. Can we talk?"

He laid a bear-sized hand on my shoulder and steered me into his private office. The Irish coffee was strong and very welcome. So was the whiskey chaser. The degenerate's way to start the day. Except that it was still yesterday for Sean.

A wealthy American, old money from Massachusetts, Sean was a massive, gentle-faced man in his early forties. If the world had been a different place in the Sixties, Sean would have been a Bostonian socialite with a seat in the U.S. Senate and Presidential ambitions. After graduating *summa cum laude* from Yale he rejected the family bank and went off to be beautiful in San Francisco. Then the horrendous mess of the Vietnam war caught up with him. Sean was there for seven years: Special Forces, clandestine operations, Intelligence — a fighting spook who came out on one of the last choppers. Those years had changed him into a man who had nightmares at breakfast time, and only slept well with a handgun by his bed and one of a long line of girls in it. The Alamo was his personalized diversion where he picked up the girls, drank heavily and underwent sessions with a psychotherapist when the flashing tracer of disco lights became too much for him.

The almost colourless eyes fixed on me and he knew the nature of my call before I spoke.

"When are you going to see the light, H?" he asked, sadly.

"Not long now. I'm retired in a day or two. Ever hear of a Bill Ives, base security at the U.S. Naval Facility at Whitesands Head down in Wales?"

He shook his grey head.

"Check with the F.B.I. at the London Embassy," he suggested. "Or is it a little too delicate for official channels?"

"Something like that. I lost an old mate recently. Ives' name has come up. Maybe in an explosive context."

Sean lit a cigarette and looked directly at me.

"I'll ask around. Give me a day."

"Thanks mate. I wouldn't ask, only this face wasn't all they tried to give me. What's at Whitesands?"

"Back-up command centre for fighting the North Atlantic approaches. Submarine warfare. Maybe something else too. I'll let you know. Watch yourself."

When I left Sean was staring into his chaser. My visit had brought it all back to him, the sabotage, the executions, the My Lais. Like me he knew that once you have played the game, you have to live with it. Until you are far enough away to forget, or until the game plays you — out for good.

Everyone says the Intelligence game is the dirtiest there is. They say it so often that it becomes boring, but that doesn't stop it being true. The more I thought about it, the more I was convinced that Verity was using me for a wider purpose than just investigating Jack Lane's death. It was time to ask Rigby a few questions.

Internal Security, who watched the watchers, were marginally less popular than herpes. Except you didn't have to get that close to them to suffer similar effects. Rigby, the chief pariah, was rumoured to be a man of unsavoury antecedents. Defrocked from the Church for offences against choirboys was the most popular legend. I put that one down to malicious historical gossip on the executive floor of S.I.S. They had never loved Rigby. Not difficult to understand why. For starters, as a much younger man he had wandered through the wilderness of Queen Anne's Gate casting aspersions on someone called Philby.

Now Rigby was an old man at sixty-four who spent hours seated by the Serpentine, his bespectacled eyes following the bright, healthy young girls jogging through the Park. He ignored the currently whispered insult going the rounds at Century House where some Oxbridge wag with a Double First and two left operational feet had christened him the Finchley Flasher. On a cold Thursday morning Rigby was alone with his innermost thoughts and a bagful of crusts for the expectant mallard. He idly lobbed a handful of bread into the water and smiled inwardly as the duck scuffled eagerly for the food.

Rigby would never change. He had been doing the same thing professionally since before I was born.

I watched him from a distance. He picked his nose for a while and then took a handkerchief from the vintage Burberry overcoat. A silver snuff box appeared from another pocket and he sniffed mightily, inclining his head backwards. Even before I walked towards him I knew he had seen me. For a moment I almost felt sad that they were retiring Rigby at the end of the month. Internal Security would never be run with the same lunatic zeal and low cunning ever again.

"Taken to snorting coke in your old age?" I asked.

Without turning around he said:

"Give my love to whoever gave you that face."

"Your people have been watching me. That's against the rules."

The low-voiced chuckle sounded like a cement mixer starting up.

"Sit next to Uncle and tell him all about it."

The vacant eyes looked at me but no further. The drooping mouth turned up at the edges into what passed for a smile. Then he blew his long nose and startled the mallard into whistling flight.

"Sloane Square," I explained. "Midnight Friday. I had Special Branch bounce them. They told Special Branch to piss off."

"So why don't you make an official complaint through your department head to my minister?"

"So why don't I just blow your balls off instead?"

Rigby raised an eyebrow as he saw my right hand deep in my coat pocket. He sniffed again.

"I'm too old to miss 'em. All in the mind at my age. What's got into you? I thought you were due off the strength tomorrow."

"Someone got Jack Lane. He was on unofficial business, officially, I think."

Rigby looked up at the darkening sky. Heavy rain-clouds loomed.

"A noble man, Jack. One of the old school. He wouldn't be sitting here talking about it. I'd be minus my equipment by now. I'll give you words of advice, between retired professionals. Leave it out. You're in murky waters. No-one was watching you specifically. No, correction. The order to keep an eye on you, temporarily, didn't entail any new disposition of manpower. The request for both surveillances came direct from my minister. First time in forty years any of the buggers have acknowledged my existence, even privately."

So it was a politically sensitive operation. I decided to try a flier, see if Rigby shot it down.

"How's Charles?"

Rigby grinned. His false teeth needed cleaning.

"I told him not to let you get the first one in."

"Thanks, Rigby."

"Come and see an old man some time."

"I will."

"And H — the people who gave you that face. Blow their balls off instead. Watch yourself. My thin water tells me you are being used."

Ames was always in his office by 8.30 sharp every morning. He had the best office in the building, mainly because he virtually lived in it. The deep pile carpet ankle-tapped you as you walked in. It didn't matter much if you fell because you would land on carpet. The desk was ten yards from the door. Made in the days when they really made desks, this one was mahogany, big enough to mount an M60 machine-gun and strong enough to take the recoil. Even the tall Ames was dwarfed by his surroundings: high bookcases packed with leather-bound histories of politics and warfare, philosophy and science, windows set high in the wall, a seven-foot coatstand, and concealed behind mahogany doors, safes and a gun cabinet.

He looked up from the report he was compiling.

"You look dreadful. Some study on stress. All hit you at once, did it?"

"I almost got killed."

Ames did not find that so funny. I knew by looking at him that he had been told less than I had. Now Ames would set you up along with the best of them, but only if it was his idea or someone had consulted him. Other people setting his section up without prior notice was treason in his eyes. And he wanted to know what had happened. So I told him some of it. Then I asked:

"How soon can you dig Jack Lane up?"

"Exhumation orders take time."

"Burke and Hare job, whatever. Just do it. Now what goes on at the U.S. Naval Facility at Whitesands Head?"

"Didn't know they had one. I'll meander over later on and buy an admiral a pink gin. What's your next move?"

"Wait for information from the Swiss. I'll see you later."

The telex girl made me more coffee. I had blown my cover to Ames because if what I suspected was true, I'd need his influence with God, or Mowlam as the Almighty was known around the Cabinet Office.

Gunther had been working hard. His information was detailed and it had arrived quickly. It usually did. The Swiss don't have inefficient dummies in their Security apparatus, and certainly not in the number three spot.

Natasha Madsen, born 1962, Berne, Switzerland. Father, the banker Henri Paul Madsen, deceased three months before his daughter was born. Maybe he didn't relish the patter of tiny feet driving him daft? No. Coronary thrombosis. Gnomes of Zurich disease. Two years later the mother, Rowena, had married a British diplomat serving in the Berne Embassy. Natasha was educated in England and at a finishing school in Berne. Where else? Aged nineteen she had started working for an outfit called the World Peace and International Friendship Foundation in Geneva.

Residence: Own apartment. Conveyance: Alfa Romeo convertible. Relationships: nothing permanent. No criminal record, no medical record of drug abuse. Travelled widely in Europe and U.S.A. Sociable girl, seen frequently at the best parties in the company of those young men with several homes and numerous bank accounts. Her own was healthy. According to Gunther she was worth half a million U.S. dollars.

Why the hell would anyone that wealthy work for a living? The report on the W.P.I.F.F. was interesting. Founded by an arms dealer who had made several fortunes out of as many wars. Par for the course. They only start the wars when trade is on the slow side. On his cancerous deathbed the old bastard suffered an attack of conscience, probably brought on by concern for his immortal soul. Deeply religious near the end, he obviously believed in insurance. So he bequeathed his ill-gotten millions to two innocent, peace-loving souls who had the ultimate solution to end all wars and promote international friendship: the West could junk all its hardware and the lovable old Soviet Union would be bound to follow suit. Their faith in human nature was greater than their benefactor's. He also bequeathed them a corporate lawyer to act as a trustee for the Fellowship now ensconced in the vacated ancestral *Schloss*. And since 1959 the W.P.I.F.F. had been spreading their message.

Any outfit like that attracts attention from the Intelligence agencies, if only out of curiosity as to its leadership's mental state. I checked the data Five had collected on the U.K. branch. Recognized members and several personnel ranged from genuine believers through to outright Communists, covering varying shades of opinion in between. Five had nothing on Natasha Madsen.

Now according to Gunther, and I'd never known him wrong, Natasha Madsen was a C.I.A. plant working inside the W.P.I.F.F. Not just guesswork, either. An on-off boyfriend ran the Company's agents in the Berne canton. Two days after her death, the local police had caught two of the Berne Station plumbers tidying up her apartment.

Which all raised a number of questions. What was a C.I.A. operative doing under the guise of a disarmament freak lurking around the vicinity of a U.S. Naval Facility? And why hadn't the C.I.A. yelled foul to Five or at least made some effort to find out how their agent had died? Instead Verity had sent Jack Lane. And that might only have been for personal reasons. At least it seemed that way to me because I had listened very carefully to the garrulous Goldstein at Verity's party. Which was where this nonsense had all started.

Chapter 11

I WENT ROUND the corner to my favourite steak house for an early lunch. Fish was supposed to be good for the brain so I started with whitebait before devouring a pound of grilled rump steak. I needed building up. The gastro-enteritis had become another unpleasant memory, like the prison cell, the warehouse, and the painful drive to Brecon.

At 2.15 pm I phoned Sean. He had not been to bed yet. Too busy asking about Bill Ives. But he had an answer, and one I didn't much like the sound of. Bill Ives used to be with the N.S.A. and specialists like him were hard to find. A few years back Ives had specialized in deep cover operations, setting up communications bases in unfriendly territory, rigging radio-stations for any U.S. approved freedom fighters from South America to South-East Asia, via the Horn of Africa and the Middle East. The word from Sean was that Ives was tops in covert communications and electronic and other methods of protecting such communications and supplies. So what was a specialist like him doing as a security policeman at a U.S. Navy base?

Ames was able to throw some light on that one. The pink gin had become lunch at the Naval and Military, with tangible results. The Admiral had done a liaison stint with U.S. Naval Intelligence and therefore realized that the N.S.A. were not some obscure do-it-yourself furniture manufacturers. In fact he knew more about their local activities than he should have done.

First the official story. Whitesands Head was a back-up command centre for co-ordinating submarine warfare to counter any Soviet threat to supply lines in the event of war in Europe. U.S. Naval Intelligence were in charge of base security. Except that the N.S.A. had a self-contained high security compound at

Whitesands, ostensibly for collecting, analysing and disseminating strategic information.

"That is all very helpful," I told Ames.

"This compound is serviced by submarine direct from the U.S., according to the Admiral. A deep navigation channel at Whitesands enables a sub to surface inside the base area without being seen from the outside. And after supplying Whitesands N.S.A. compound it heads west."

"Where to?" I asked.

"West coast of Eire. The N.S.A. have another facility there."

"Micks are neutral," I countered. "They only fight amongst themselves."

"Not according to the Admiral. So where does that leave us?"

"I'm going upstairs. Call me when you get the autopsy report on Jack."

I met the secretary with the report on the stairs. She wouldn't give the thin folder to me. Not surprising. I am so rarely in the office that even the building security people check my pass three times. I settled myself in Ames' armchair while he scanned the papers. The look on his face was serious.

"According to this, Jack was full of anticholinergic drugs, hyoscine hydrobromide, whatever that is."

"Anticholinergics," I explained, "are used by the medicos to dry bronchial and salivary secretions increased by intubations and inhalational anaesthetics, and to prevent excessive bradycardia and hypotension caused by halothane etcetera."

Ames looked at me as if I had flipped.

"Substitute the word scopolamine for hyoscine hydrobromide and you have a drug that is used to treat amnesia."

"Or to obtain the truth from an uncooperative person," Ames added. He was with it now.

"In excess doses it is dangerous. Slows the heart rate alarmingly."

"How the hell did you know that?" he asked.

"I used to sleep with a pharmacist whose only interests were chemistry and sex. They used chloral hydrate in my whisky which put me out like a light. Side effects of that stuff are gastro-intestinal

81

disturbances but we won't talk about my insides. So, they shot Jack full of truth serum. How did Jack break his leg?"

"Manner consistent with a fall?" Ames suggested.

"Or someone broke it for him. Any bruises around the kidney area?"

Ames nodded.

"Someone hitting him where it wouldn't show. Jack was too tough to crack so they put a specialist on him with a hypo. Bastards. I'm going out now. Then I'll call Verity for a meet tonight. He's got some explaining to do. Bring Mowlam along. I need some clout on this one."

I sat in the car, waiting. And while I waited I knew that Jack's death was not a simple case of murder, perpetrated or covered up by some local mafia. It was much bigger than that.

The N.S.A. covered many dodgy areas. Its beat was worldwide, like our very own G.C.H.Q. at Cheltenham, only better at keeping its own secrets and covering up its own leaks. The 1947 American National Security Act had brought the National Security Agency into being. It was responsible to the National Security Council which advised the White House on political and global strategy. The N.S.A.'s function was to maintain U.S. Intelligence communications worldwide and listen in on everyone else's.

Forget the old days when you just wired a room or tapped a couple of individual phones. The N.S.A. could monitor all the transatlantic phone circuits, the radio traffic and the telexes in an area the size of Europe simultaneously. Twelve acres of computers at a place called Fort Meade in Maryland searched this traffic for key words, and they could search at phenomenal speed, millions of words a second.

This mass surveillance was targeted according to categorized watching briefs, updated hourly. It watched the press, radio and television output, and all the communications to and from political parties, trade unions, embassies, terrorist groups and governments. It noted commercial deals and banking discussions. So next time you use the head office phone to call the extra-marital entertainment from the branch down the road, remember, the

N.S.A. or the G.C.H.Q. have the capacity to hear your guilty secrets. The N.S.A. will most likely keep them, on file. G.C.H.Q. have been known to snitch, so you could be named in the gossip columns of *Pravda* or *Izvestia*.

Not that the N.S.A. was just computers. They had agents watching the worldwide network of bases and listening posts. These guys would keep tabs on their own personnel, mingle with those who didn't like them, and maybe discourage those who got too nosey. And some of these people had links with the Pentagon and the big conglomerates, to ensure themselves highly-paid second careers when they had done their stint for Uncle Sam.

Outfits like the N.S.A. were always a problem. They could be a law unto themselves. And there was usually one man somewhere using the organization for his own or someone else's benefit. Bill Ives worked for the N.S.A.

And Bo Pepper worked for the C.I.A. His teeth were the first thing you saw in the dark. The rest of him was ebony black. The dark overcoat covered his light-grey suit so that he mingled easily with the dark shadows. I opened the car door for him. Fifty yards down the street an Audi saloon waited, sidelights on, two men up front. Bo had brought his minders.

"Why the rush, Halloran, and what's wrong with my office?"

Pepper was not one of the Company's street negroes. He was a lawyer by training, and by inclination a man who liked the creature comforts of his Grosvenor Square Office, just to the right of the eagle. The C.I.A. do operate in Britain, the same as anywhere else. We like to think they tell us some of what they are up to. They like us to think they do. It's called the special relationship.

"Natasha Madsen, Swiss national, fell to her death at a Christmas party in Wales. One of yours, I think."

Bo kept his mouth shut, fiddled around with a pack of cigarettes and shook his head.

"There are proper channels for enquiries of this nature. Use them," he finally advised.

"So why haven't you put in an official request for an investigation? Or at least made your own enquiries?"

"Ask Langley."

"I can't afford the plane fare out there."

"Is this official?" Bo asked, looking sideways at me.

"Sure. That's why you're freezing your black arse in a car with a heater that doesn't work down in Bermondsey. You've never been to Bermondsey before."

"You let this out, Halloran and you'll be freezing your white arse off twenty feet under the Thames. Natasha Madsen was working under direct orders from Langley. No local support. This was a Deputy Director-level decision. So was the order not to investigate."

"Because she was undercover in the area of a highly sensitive N.S.A. base? Some kind of inter-agency fight brewing?"

"All I know is that they sent an inexperienced kid with a cover employment likely to get her hurt into that highly sensitive area. Don't ask why. I don't know. But I do know this, you stick your nose in and you will end up in the river. Leave Uncle Sam to chastise his own."

"Thank you for your encouragement Bo."

"Up yours, Halloran."

Very unlawyer-like of Bo. But I appreciated his warning and he knew I had got the message. The Star Chamber types across the Atlantic were at it as well.

I stopped in the local pub half a mile from chez Verity. I needed to collect my thoughts, and have a large one to steady my nerves. At ten pm, in less than half an hour, I was due to ask some awkward questions. Verity owed me an explanation.

When I arrived, five minutes early, the butler did not answer the door. It must have been his night off. I was not the only visitor. A Bentley Mulsanne Turbo was parked in front of the house and there was no sign of Ames' car.

Lady Davinia answered the door. I liked her even better in tight jeans and a skinny sweater. She still looked about nineteen and smiled at me. I did like her smile. She politely omitted to enquire after my obviously battered face. Then I supposed she came from a long line of diplomats. She pointed me in the direction of the library and disappeared up the stairs. Given a choice in the matter

I would rather have gone with her. Because as I walked through the library door the sociable joviality of the assembled company became an awkward silence. Ames said only:

"Hello, Halloran."

His poker face told me the other two had been conspiring in my absence. Verity smiled amiably. I didn't trust him when he smiled. He too was dressed in jeans and a sweater. He would have looked better in pinstripes. Then the school swot stare fixed on me as he said:

"I don't believe you know Sir Maurice Mowlam."

Fatuous remark. Of course I didn't. How many vicars have actually met God? I knew who Mowlam was: the keeper of all secrets, the chief conspirator of the Star Chamber. He ran the Joint Intelligence Committee. The Prime Minister listened to Mowlam and had, by all accounts, started to take the advice.

Verity handed me a Waterford of his best malt. Slippery and sneaky he might be. Mean with his whisky he was not. I sat down, as invited. Mowlam looked at me as though I were an example of some hitherto unknown species of wildlife about to be stuffed and exhibited. I lit a cigarillo and felt undergunned. So I gritted my teeth silently. The adrenaline started pumping. I sipped my whisky and stared straight back at Mowlam.

Mowlam actually looked like a conspirator. Not a muscle moved in his thin, anorexic face. Sunken eyes stared coldly at me. The lines on his narrow forehead were etched deep into his pale skin. Bony fingers curled around the whisky glass. I knew he was no older than fifty-five. I'd have hated to be seventy looking like he did. Yet there was fire in those eyes, iced fire and I knew by looking at him that I was in the frozen spotlight of intense scrutiny. Not a comforting feeling.

"I don't like being used, Verity," I spoke quietly. Never shout at people like these. It makes them think you're worried. Then they smell blood.

"Do elaborate," Mowlam invited, his voice crisp and decisive. So it was his show. He managed to make the invitation sound like a threat.

"Jack Lane's death was no accident. But you probably knew

that all along, didn't you? Because you checked the records. You sent him unofficial, Verity, to investigate your stepdaughter's death. Natasha Madsen was your stepdaughter. You were based at the Berne Embassy in the early Sixties."

I watched Verity's reaction. He swallowed hard, not out of embarrassment at being caught out but to control some emotion. I didn't give him time to dwell on the obvious grief he felt.

"When Jack didn't make it, you needed another patsy. You checked the records and my name came up in conjunction with Jack's. Conveniently, I was due for retirement. So if I ballsed it up I was deniable. I can't quite understand why you sent the cleaners to sanitize Jack's office and his flat. Presumably you had Internal Security start that little brawl at the party and keep watch on Lucinda's flat to see if I was as good as I was made out to be. I am."

"Very astute of you," Mowlam cut in. "What exactly did you discover?"

I had the idea that I was talking to a computer that knew all the answers.

"Jack didn't die on the mountains, he was murdered. The cover-up was engineered by the local mafia named Gwyn, a relative in the police and probably ordered by a man named William Ives."

"You've been down there, I take it?" Verity asked.

"My alter ego has. He almost got killed."

"Would you give us some more details and your analysis?" Mowlam asked.

"Are you sitting comfortably? Then I'll begin. Jack went down to Glyntywyn using the inspection of the Llanmartin base as cover. Ignore those reports saying he was still there on Wednesday the fifteenth. They were covering for him and they meant well. In my view, Jack was snatched some time on the Tuesday after spending the previous night with Elizabeth Gwyn, sister-in-law of Garth who owns the house where Natasha died. He was worked over and shot full of scopolamine, not exactly corrupt local mafia style, I think you'll agree. Jack might or might not have talked but assume your brief to him is blown, Verity. Jack either died of heart failure from drug overdose or they put him in a deep freeze until the next cold spell hit the mountains. Not long to wait during January. A visit he made to the Willows, the Gwyns' club, was covered up. The hotel he stayed in is owned by the Gwyns but I don't think they are the real villains."

I took another sip of Scotch. Mowlam lit a thin cigar and never took his eyes off me.

"I went to the Willows, saw Elizabeth, and mentioned Jack's name. She feigned respectable-married-woman-cheating-on-her-husband routine but set me up. They spiked my booze at the hotel and I woke up in a police cell. I am not sure of the next part. My cover must have held up because the cops offered me a stay-out-of-town deal in return for not bringing mythical charges of assault and criminal damage. So I took the deal and a taxi brought for me. The next thing I knew two hard men were doing a clog dance on my head. One was the bull-necked copper from the local nick. The other one I cannot describe but he had a familiar feel about him. He was a pro and I know him from somewhere. And he was the angel who slugged me with a gun, a familiar gun, Jack Lane's Browning."

"He wasn't supposed to have one," Verity observed.

"People who brief me are supposed to tell the truth," I replied. "When I came around, my car was waiting conveniently outside. Someone had planted a very sophisticated bomb in it. Not the usual ignition or contact detonated job but a timing or heat activated device which used the heat of the car engine. I chucked it in the river, along with my suitcase. Always play safe. Now either they tried to sucker me into driving off and bang, or a hardcore conspiracy wanted me dead without the Gwyns and the local police knowing."

"But you're a hard man to kill." Ames grinned, almost proudly. I noticed he was wearing his old school tie.

"Now Bill Ives, who was present at the party where Natasha died, is masquerading as Base Security Officer at Whitesands Head. That's Naval Intelligence's job. Ives used to be with the N.S.A. Whitesands contained an N.S.A. compound. Ives' speciality used to be setting up advanced communication bases in hostile territory."

"They know who my lunch guest was," Ames advised me.

"So you know the whisper about an N.S.A. base in Eire supplied from Whitesands. London Station C.I.A. were forbidden on orders from Langley to investigate Natasha's death. I was told it was Uncle Sam's business. Anyone for an unsupported theory?"

Mowlam was on to his second cigar.

"By all means."

"Ives has got something on the Gwyns. They're his first line of defence. Old security trick. The K.G.B. do it all the time, informers within fifty miles of the Iron Curtain each way. Either Ives is being naughty on his own account, which explains the C.I.A. sending Natasha, or the Yanks are behind him in the cover-up of both deaths. Otherwise, Sir Maurice, they would have come to you eating humble pie pleading mistaken executive action over Jack's death and promising not to do it again."

"Interesting theory," Mowlam admitted.

"The really unkind part was sending me in. I think it was your intention to let me take Ives out. Which was the reason for your officially transferring me to the study on stress. You can then plead to the Yanks that I was always a bit of a psychopath. I crippled people during fights at parties. You thought the course had stabilized me but when I'm let loose in retirement I hear that my old mate Jack has been taken out and I go a bit loopy. You're not very nice people, are you?"

Everything went quiet. Ames was looking at the ceiling, trying not to laugh. The street survivors, with the help of Ames from the hall of mirrors, had put one over on the Star Chamber. Three cheers for Halloran! Bang goes my pension, but so what? The manipulators had been caught out playing their dirty tricks.

Verity topped my glass up and smiled.

"I'd like to play chess against you some time."

"You already did. I won."

Mowlam put his glass down and looked straight at me. This time I was really worried. I had beaten him at his own game and he seemed like a poor loser.

"What would be your reaction if I said you now retire and handed you your pension cheque?" he asked.

No, he had beaten me at my game. He knew what my answer would be. I said quietly:

"Invest my pension cheque in a lot of ammunition. You know that if Jack had still been an operational member of the section I would go out and nail the bastard who killed him. You looked on knowingly blind when that happened in the past."

"Let's trade, Halloran."

"What?" I asked.

"You have a curious instinct for knowing when you are being used. So I'll tell you the truth. I want to have a talk with Mr Ives, not personally you understand but through Verity's people. We need to know what N.S.A. thinking is on certain topics and Ives is well placed to advise us. I'll trade him immunity for Lane's death if he'll answer some questions. Bring him in alive but make it look like that personal crusade. Quite frankly I don't much care what happens to the others involved but don't involve the police. Do we have a deal?"

It sounded more like an ultimatum to me. He wanted Ives alive. And on reflection, an Ives at the mercy of a devious skeleton like Mowlam seemed more fitting retribution than a forty-one bullet where it hurt.

I thought about it. It seemed like the only game in town as the gambler said. And I could always go back on my word. Maybe it would be for the first time. And Mowlam could always go back on his, obviously for the umpteenth time.

"Agreed in principle."

"You realize of course that if Ives calls for help from his people we can't cover you."

"The possibility had crossed my mind."

Old Ames was throwing me dangerous looks. Verity noticed and flick-knifed a warning glance in his direction.

"I'll need some equipment. Ames will provide that."

Mowlam nodded. Then it was Verity's turn to stick his oar in.

"We will also need a secure channel of communication. Lucinda will do very nicely. I believe you've established something of a secure alibi with her already."

"What I do with my spare time is my concern. I'm retired, remember?"

"She would like you to call her. I'll explain the situation to her now. Then I'll hand you the telephone and you can make your own personal arrangements."

Verity left the room. For the first time, Mowlam smiled. I preferred it when he stared at me.

Verity sidled up to me as I left.

"Lucinda is expecting you for coffee."

Chapter 12

AMES WANTED A lift back to London, probably an excuse for him to have a private word. He hated my MG, and not only because the ageing soft top let in unnecessary draughts. About four years back he had bought one, complete with an original set of wire wheels, engine in first-rate condition and perfect bodywork. Then Mrs Ames made life hell for him. She thought he was being ridiculous, a middle-aged man trying to relive his youth through the fantasy of a teenager's toy. He ought to drive something more in keeping with his status, like a Mercedes saloon. Mrs Ames had been very keen on status. He told me once she had wanted him to be a general. So Ames sold the car. Twelve months later he traded in his wife. She had been reliving her youthful fantasies with her tennis coach.

Ames' lean face looked granite hard, outlined by the headlights of oncoming traffic. He lit a cigarette and said:

"I'd like to have seen you finish in one piece. You are entitled to walk now, you know. Why won't you?"

I had been asking myself the same question and come up with a variety of answers. None was the real one. But if the truth was a one-line response, many learned men throughout history had been wasting their time.

Reasons for not quitting. One: debt to Jack Lane. I had neglected him. And if the situation had been reversed, Jack would have done the same for me. Two: pride in finishing the job. Three: put one over on the Mowlams of this world. Why should they have it all their own conspiratorial way? Four: no-one kicked me to pieces, tried to kill me and walked around to talk about it. Five: a naïve and foolish reason maybe, but I didn't see why people like me and Jack should break our backs so that people like the Gwyns could screw an imperfect system to their own advantage, pushing ordinary people like Susan around.

"Because I'm ever so slightly unbalanced, Ames."

"This conversation never took place, and I have no inside knowledge to rationalize my instincts, but Mowlam is using you. Ives will run for cover and call out the U.S. cavalry to protect him. You won't have a prayer. You're another body to be used like Jack was. Mowlam is probably doing some dodgy political deal with the Americans and needs a pair of dead aces up his sleeve. You can see that, can't you?"

"Trust me, Ames. I'm the Headhunter, remember?"

"I'll write that on the label of your wreath."

"No cremation, please. With my alcohol intake the flash would be worse than Hiroshima."

Ames thought that was funny. Then he always did have a black sense of humour.

"What do you need, H?" he asked, as I slowed the MG and pulled over behind a taxi rank.

"Thought you'd never ask. Untraceable, fully equipped vehicle at this time and location tomorrow. Check it over yourself." I handed him a note with directions. Then:

"One other thing. I might need to get in touch again. So go for your customary ale at your local alone for the next few days. If followed, abort to the nearest off-licence and take a bottle home."

"Do you know something I don't?"

I deliberately left the question unanswered and drove away.

The lovely Lucinda was listening to the Brandenburg Concerto No. 1 when I arrived at her flat. Internal Security were no longer in evidence outside. I am always suspicious of people who appreciate

Bach. They sometimes want you to think they like the structured form of the music and don't realize the insight it contains.

"Very comfortable," I observed, noting the quality furnishings, the wallpaper and curtain match and the circular sofa she adorned so stylishly.

"I like it," she smiled, kissing me lightly on the cheek before handing me a glass of whisky.

"Who did that to your poor face?" she asked, concerned.

"Someone who thought it didn't fit."

I took off my jacket and unslung the Magnum. Lying back on that cushioned sofa I realized how comfortable life could be. Lucinda's brown eyes were laughing. She lay beside me, resting on her elbow, long black hair falling loosely over the shoulders of a short black dressing gown.

"But you did outmanoeuvre Simon after spotting his game plan. I think that was clever of you."

"Thanks for warning me in advance."

"Thanks for telling me where you've been," she countered. "I've been expecting you to call, if only to report on your progress."

"For the last five years I have operated alone and I've managed to stay alive. Don't feel insulted or neglected because I didn't keep in touch."

She started nibbling my ear. I slipped my hand inside her dressing gown. She moaned expectantly:

"Come and see my shower."

Nothing moved in Sloane Square before 6 am and I was away from Lucinda's flat by 5.30 am. It was the day that Halloran officially retired and ostensibly he was going on vacation. I went back to the flat to pack some things.

As I put the key in the back door I thought I had even fooled Moshe Dayan. But you never fool cats. They are psychic. Moshe was watching me from behind a dustbin. Instead of running up to meet me he waited until the last possible moment before I closed the door to start his home run.

"I reckon you know what's going on."

He made a conspiratorial, cat-like noise and followed me into the kitchen. I made coffee and he asked for milk. There wasn't any. So he lapped reluctantly at the dish of water. I went into the lounge in search of some cigarillos and sat down on the sofa. Moshe jumped up beside me and sat, purring heavily, eyelids half-closed.

"You want me to tell you."

He answered with a brief miaow.

"Pay attention then, you crafty cat, and tell me how this sounds. Mowlam wants Ives, so we give him Ives. How? I'll tell you. I had the impression that Elizabeth Gwyn trapped me somewhat unwillingly. She kept saying how sorry she was when I hit the floor. Before that she let on that Superintendent Daniels didn't like Ives very much, because Ives knew what was going on. So I'll gently blackmail the Gwyns into setting up Ives for a snatch. Great idea, eh?"

Moshe Dayan did not seem over-impressed.

"We'll see who scares the Gwyns most, me or Ives. It won't be easy, but it won't be as difficult as breaking into that N.S.A. compound to drag him out by the scruff of his neck. Agreed?"

Moshe Dayan was still not ecstatic. His one good eye regarded me from under a sleepy eyelid.

"But first we have to split the players up. We have to find the weakness in the Gwyns' organization and lean on the witnesses who gave evidence at the Natasha Madsen inquest. A sound first move, I believe."

That damned cat was no longer listening. He was asleep on the sofa. Ironic. The only one I could trust to keep his mouth shut about my plans was not paying any kind of attention.

I packed a suitcase and put the cat out of the back door. He looked indignantly at me.

"Work for a living," I ordered. "Mind the shop."

But he was no longer there. That ungrateful cat had gone tomming it again.

I had not driven far when I knew I had a tail. The Volkswagen Polo followed me for three streets, tucked in the line of traffic next but one vehicle behind me. Then an old Mini took over. I doubled back the way I had come with the Mini still behind me. More ring-around-the-houses and a taxi took over. Instinct told me all the vehicles were working as a team.

Now a proper tail job is an expensive operation, requiring co-ordination and anything up to thirty vehicles. Once a follower has been clocked he is useless. You should never run the same vehicle for more than a mile in city traffic. The follower can't hang too far back otherwise he'll lose the target vehicle. The best method of all is a bleeper. Fixed to the target vehicle it transmits signals for up to five miles, sometimes more. While useless for observing a meet or the antics of a target vehicle's occupants, it is the most discreet way of discovering a destination.

I joined the M1 and the Volkswagen rejoined the tag game. Suddenly that old Mini was in front of me and I realized I was boxed in because a motorbike had drawn level with me, occupying the middle lane. Both driver and pillion passenger were leathered up and wore white helmets with dark visors.

The motorbike made no attempt to pass me and my heart started jumping the odd beat while my stomach felt weak. The Volkswagen was close behind me now, two men up front. The Mini in front of me had two up, with one man in the back looking out of the rear window at me.

It looked like a trap and at sixty miles an hour I could do nothing about it. Pinned in on three sides, unable to defend myself and drive, I was a sitting target for the pillion passenger on the bike, the man in the back of the Mini, or the front passenger in the Polo.

I gripped the steering wheel with my left hand and slid my right hand across to grab the Magnum from the holster. I held the gun with one hand in my lap. This was a lunatic's game. Any moment now there could be a pile up and I would be strawberry sandwiches right in the middle of it. Suddenly the motorbike accelerated away, weaving in and out of the vehicles ahead of me. Now was a chance and I changed down to third gear to break out.

Too late. A Chevette had taken the place of the motorbike. As I glanced across to the passenger seat I could see a face as black as ebony grinning at me from that Chevette. It was Bo Pepper and in his hands was an Uzi sub-machine-gun.

Speed along a motorway over the limit and the world is full of traffic cops. Get caught in real trouble and you never see a sign of them.

Bo was enjoying himself, flashing toothpaste-commercial grins at me. Suddenly, he hung back and the cars in front and behind me fell away another twenty yards. I put my foot to the floorboards and pulled out. Pepper's Chevette tried to give me a race. The MG rattled and shuddered as the needle swung quickly over the ninety mark and kept on climbing.

I had bought the car second-hand. The bodywork was like mine, ageing and dented here and there. But the engine was in first-class order. The motor pool mechanics kept it that way. Pepper's family car was ideal for following families, but not for chasing a frightened and angry Halloran in his wire-wheeled, middle-aged teenage machine.

Ten miles on I had left them all behind and there was no sign of the motorbike. The exit road enabled me to double back to Dunstable. Following the B489 along the edge of the Chilterns I kept my eyes open all round me until I joined the A41. I turned right through Aylesbury and drove on as far as Oxford. With any luck, Bo would imagine I was heading north.

It did not make any sense to me. That black joker could have killed me on the motorway. Instead he waved and gave me one of his stupid, superior smiles. They had tailed me from the flat where it would have been very easy to take me out as I walked out of the back door. He was trying to tell me something.

Ames had got it right. The big Volvo estate car was waiting in the municipal car park. Its driver was a young, earnest civil service type. We exchanged briefcases and car keys without a word being spoken. He drove off in the MG and I waited the statutory two minutes before leaving in the opposite direction.

Driving that Volvo was like handling a truck after the MG. But the Volvo had its advantages, like hardened steel bodywork and bullet-resistant glass, electronically-tuned engine and two-way multi-channelled radio which could eavesdrop on any police or emergency service frequency. In addition, there was also a C.B. set.

I made some phone calls from the local police headquarters. I carried an identification card which stated my name was James Halloran and I was a Superintendent of Scotland Yard's Special Branch. I gave the local brass the brush-off and was given an office and an outside line for two hours. The coffee was undrinkable but the tea was good and I spent ten minutes chatting up an attractive blonde W.P.C. who brought it. My phone calls finished, I drove off down the A40.

I was in the Blue Bell in Brecon by opening time and Frank had been as good as his word. Bill Islwyn Evans was in the lounge bar and when he caught sight of me his heavy features turned greyer than his suit. Then he rounded aggressively on Frank.

"You bastard. Come up for a night out, you said."

"Won't take long Bill. You know the way to Frank's sitting-room. I'll get the drinks. And don't try to leave via the Gents."

Frank looked solemnly at me.

"At this rate I won't have any friends left," he grumbled.

Frank's living room was private. Even the cat left. Islwyn Evans fingered his brandy nervously and looked around for signs of comfort. I gave him a cigarillo to calm him down.

"They call me Halloran. Frank will tell you I'm straight and that I'm only the meanest bastard on two feet so you have no worries. Breathe a word of what we discuss and I'll bang you up on an Official Secrets charge for so long you'll only come out for your funeral. If you need protection, compensation or even relocation I can arrange it with one phone call. I can also muster enough clout to piss over the Glyntywyn police in public and have their Chief Constable thank me. Understand the ground rules?"

I had to play it hard and fast because if I let up on him he might think about repercussions, to his friends, his business or even his pet canary, if he told me anything about the Gwyns.

"If you're such a hard man, who gave you that face?"

Like Jack Lane used to say, there is always some smart arse with a clever question.

"Very perceptive, William. I got bounced by two of your policemen. Being pig-trough ignorant and not checking my real identity, they made the biggest mistake of their dreary little lives in

96

setting me up for a kicking. I am about to return the compliment. First question. Bull-necked, deep-voiced anthropoid in plain-clothes who likes hitting suspects. Name?"

Islwyn Evans swallowed hard, then:

"Detective Sergeant Ieuan Ellis, a real rough handful."

"Not for long. Next. His brown-eyed, soft-shoed chum. Dark hair, dark moustache, early twenties. He plays the nice guy."

"Sounds like young Delme Owens. I didn't think he was one of them."

"That's his problem. Now Jack Lane came to you for information. What did you tell him?"

"Nothing specific, just the general rumours and what I knew about the Gwyns. Worst mistake I ever made. I thought he would keep his mouth shut. He obviously didn't. Two days later there was a fight in my lounge bar. I never have fights in my pub. This was rent-a-crowd stuff. The bloody police waited outside until the place was wrecked. Then they didn't arrest anyone. Ellis called round next day and took me to one side for a friendly chat. Keep my opinions to myself in future, or the breathalysers would be waiting at the entrance to my car park. Then of course there would be a visit every night at stop tap and the next trouble I had might force the police to object to my licence being renewed. He pointed out that a lot of 999 calls were hoaxes and redecoration was expensive. People didn't like to drink where there was trouble. But I can't prove it because there were no witnesses to our conversation."

"Jack Lane tried to keep his mouth shut. But they broke him down with truth serum. The poor bastard spilled out anything. Which probably explains the visit."

Islwyn Evans looked concerned. He was about to waver. His eyes asked me if I would break the same way.

"They missed their chance with me, Bill. Now you give me as much background information as you can. Then we'll borrow Frank's typewriter and I'll type out your statement of complaint about Ellis's behaviour which I will add to my own. Then the Chief Constable can have fun dismissing those guilty from the force and putting them on trial."

That did it. Islwyn Evans stood up, shouted at me, and tried a rush for the door. It took me ten minutes to convince him of my sincerity during which time I deliberately let him see my gun and my Blue Pass. His confidence was boosted. Then I sat like a good interrogator should and listened, at the same time as typing out the statement with my clumsy fingers.

As I drove away I went over Islwyn Evans's story in my mind. The bent had become a way of life in Glyntywyn. Alan and Garth Gwyn had built on a late father's honest toil and turned everything the old man had worked for rotten.

The system was almost as old as the Black Mountains where they had dumped Jack's body. The Gwyns got all the council contracts for their building companies. Roads, construction and mainten- ance. On the private side, they never had any trouble getting planning permissions. They were screwing the council for money using the tried and tested routine of inflating the administrative costs, cheating on the road specifications and the building regulations. Any quality control inspectors were bribed into agreement. And if that didn't work someone usually had his arm broken in a street brawl or had his family threatened by an anonymous phone caller. On one occasion the sanctions had been taken as far as setting fire to someone's house. The police investigation blamed short-sighted holiday home arsonists.

The Willows was a useful channel for dispensing untraceable favours to local authority members and employees. Gambling credit, holidays and the occasional female company were all available. The Gwyns were an astute tribe. They socialized with all the right people and Alan Gwyn even sat on the local Bench. They supported all the charities and gave generously to local events.

But they were also mixed up in Jack Lane's death. And I wanted them for it.

Chapter 13

JACK LANE ALWAYS used to say: "Protect your sources of information. If you have to disclose them, make sure you scare the hell out of whoever is left to take revenge on them. No matter what they think in the Star Chamber, sources are never expendable."

Jack was right. His advice was motivated partly by expediency but mainly by conscience. That was always his problem, his conscience. I had the same problem. Deep down, carefully concealed from public view, but never totally suppressible, I had a conscience too. Not an advantage in my line of work. My business was transacted in a jungle where the rule of law was abrogated in favour of personal survival. Whichever other side you happened to be up against, and that usually meant everyone else, the only rule was: 'Be on your feet at the end of the day.' Jack rationalized this breaking the rules of civilized behaviour quite simply. "We're one of the reasons everyone else has the freedom to be overtaxed, fed a load of bullshit, be unemployed, without thinking too carefully about how they are able to enjoy those luxuries."

Jack was probably right about that too. The Gwyns were essentially a side show to the main objective of William Ives but they still had to be scared silly. I needed some witnesses to enable me to discover in detail what actually happened. And I'd have to protect them. With one of me and innumerable opposition I'd be spreading myself thin on the ground.

It was who-owes-Halloran-a-favour-time. Shortlist of one. Barrett at Llanmartin. I telephoned him, reminded him that he owed me his job and gave him some arrangements to make. From the same payphone I called Elizabeth Gwyn because she was the real short-cut to the manner of Jack's death. The au pair told me she had gone on holiday, Mr Gwyn had not gone with her this time and no, she had no idea where Mrs Gwyn was.

Maybe her husband had sent her away. Maybe she had left him. I only knew that she had been scared when I approached her at the Willows. Probably afraid of her husband. He didn't look the forgiving type. Severe streak of righteous Methodism in his family, no doubt.

So it was time to look for Susan, the girl who had been worried about her job at the Lion and her child. I wanted a statement from her about Jack leaving the Lion on Tuesday 14 January. Then maybe I could provoke J. C. Daniels into doing a deal with me to save his job.

She was behind the bar when I walked in at 10.15. The Lion's guests that night couldn't have been much of a drinking crowd because the bar was almost empty. Her big blue eyes looked nervously away as I said:

"Hello, Susan."

She looked around her desperately, to see if anyone was watching.

"What do you want?" she demanded. "If they see you here . . . "

"Small Scotch and a few words with you, alone. What time do you finish?"

I showed her the Special Branch warrant card that identified me as Detective Superintendent James Halloran. She looked up at me disbelievingly.

"I finish at eleven-thirty. I've told you. I can't get involved . . . "

"Where do you live? Or would you prefer I asked the management for your address?"

The poor girl looked betrayed. Nervous eyes accused me of worse crimes than murder. Reluctantly she scribbled her address on the back of a card.

"I'll be along later. Now whatever happens, don't panic."

I took her hand and held it for a moment. When I turned to walk out, Adamson came into the bar. Didn't this guy have an office to hide in?

He recognized me very clearly. His mouth twitched nervously and he smiled foolishly. I seized him by his lapels and shoved him hard against the wall. He was breathing in short, sharp spasms.

"You've just lost a star rating," I grinned. "The gourmet guide people know about the lousy Scotch your room service dispenses. I told them."

I smiled at Susan and walked away. Adamson wasn't worth the physical effort of a slap across the face. I walked into the foyer, made another call from the payphone, then disappeared into the night.

A good operative must be able to improvise. It was unfortunate that Adamson had seen me because he was probably on the phone to his boss at that very moment. Still, that was life, and no-one ever said it would be easy. So, the Gwyns would know I was still in one piece and had been talking to Susan. Their course of action would be to talk to Susan, ask her what I wanted, and then warn her off at the very least. Always protect your sources, and especially if they haven't given you all the information yet. It was time to hang around and make sure the girl arrived home safely.

I waited in the shadows of the hotel car park and from there I could observe all arrivals and departures. It was street time now. Glyntywyn streets these might be, but they were my streets. Because the streets were where I worked, where I sought my quarry and where I hid when the tables were turned. I knew every shadow cast by every street lamp ever made. I knew where to stand so you could see me and where to stand so you could not, until it was too late. I knew the places car headlights never illuminated and every sound of the traffic-filled night. I knew a blind alley before walking into it and instinct told me the difference between a cul-de-sac and a through side road.

I could follow an expert for half a mile and still have him think I was the town drunk. I could stand on a street corner doing nothing for hours and still do it convincingly. So, the next time you see a slept-in face topped with thinning hair standing in your bus queue, think about it. That face might be checking the time, absorbed in a local paper, smoking a cigarillo expectantly or working out where it ought to be with the aid of a street map. That face could be me. And I could be following you. And even if you suspected you were being followed or watched, you'd look right through me because I fitted neatly in to your familiar surroundings.

The night was cloudy and damp, the air heavy with what was almost a fine rain. The pavements echoed to the sound of late-night pedestrian drunks wending their loud way homeward. Why do people have to shout when they're loaded? A young couple came tottering out of the hotel, arm in arm, and stood not ten feet from me. They entwined and started eating each other. He had his hand up her skirt but she was against sex in a public place. She preferred the back seat of a car in some deserted country lane. He had difficulty getting his key into the car doorlock. She giggled and told him he would have to do better than that later on. They drove off without realizing anyone had even heard them.

The night sounds quietened. The traffic had tailed off, the laughing had subsided. I wanted a cigarillo but that would have to wait. Flickering flame of a lighter or even the dull glow of a cigarette betrays your presence. A good man will always spot either. An expert can smell tobacco smoke, even on a damp night with its carbon monoxide fumes and numerous other smells.

It was now 11.50 and Susan was late. I was thinking about going in for her or maybe giving her another ten minutes when the clicking of nervous heels told me she was on the way. Halfway along the street she stopped, looked all around her and then walked on, her pace quickening insistently. I followed.

The easiest way for anyone to take her would be on the streets. No witnesses. I slipped the safety thong off the holster of the forty-one Magnum. Probably a car snatch so I closed the distance between us to thirty yards and listened out for any approaching or passing vehicles. At the same time I paid particular attention to the interior of anything parked.

The main streets became side roads. I had one anxious moment when a wayward character approached her from behind a parked car. No other support in sight. Hell! Just my luck for the neighbourhood rapist to have chosen her as a victim. No. He only wanted to know the time. As he came towards me I could smell the beer on his breath five yards away. He never saw me because he was singing to himself.

The side road ran into a darkened alley. Now alleys are always a problem, narrow and often with no recesses to dodge into. Also, if trouble does materialize, one good street fighter at each end and you are surrounded easily. Susan's footsteps quickened. Mine made no sound. I kept looking over my shoulder for signs of someone cutting off the retreat. No. All clear. I relaxed a little.

We were now in a dimly-lit side street, narrow, with terraced cottages on either side. Some had been boarded up. Not the best part of town. And fifty yards along, a police car was parked beneath the pale-yellow light of an old street lamp. A uniformed copper was leaning on the car, enjoying a smoke in company with a plainclothes man. As Susan approached, they blocked her way. So the Gwyns were using the police.

"A word, love, inside. Give me your house keys," the plain-clothes man ordered. I recognized his voice. My brown-eyed friend from the interrogation room, Delme Owens.

I slid into a doorway as the uniformed man grabbed Susan's arm.

"Don't argue, love. Get inside."

I held back until the door slammed shut. Then I moved up to the police car, a white Fiesta panda, and noted its number. It was safe to light a cigarillo now. Suddenly the door of Susan's house opened. A dumpy, headscarved woman stumped out into the street, took one look at me and tottered off as fast as she could go on short, thick-stockinged legs.

I listened at the door. From inside came the sounds of raised voices and a child crying. Then a stifled scream. It was time I had a look at what was going on. So I leaned heavily on the doorbell. After a minute or so a heavy, awkward young copper answered the door.

"What do you want?" he demanded.

I flashed the Special Branch warrant card in his face.

"Shift your fat self," I ordered.

His lopsided face was even less attractive when confused. I barged past his bulk, not an easy task in the narrow hallway. Inside a small, sparsely furnished sitting room, Delme Owens was busy wrecking the furniture, ornaments and anything else he could lay his hands on. Susan was holding a wide-eyed, curly headed toddler in her arms. The child was screaming.

"Go away. You hurt Mummy."

Owens stared incredulously at my warrant card.

"Never make snap judgements on first impressions," I smiled. Then I rounded on the uniformed lout.

"Go and play policemen somewhere, simple Simon. I've got your number for when I require you again."

It dawned on my awkward friend that his future was in serious doubt. He looked expectantly at Owens.

"Move it, fatso," I snapped. "Or I'll have your warrant card now."

He shuffled awkwardly off. I moved for the telephone and dialled a local number. All the recipient needed was a one-line instruction.

"Halloran. Go to phase one."

Owens looked grey. I smiled.

"I can explain this, sir." His mouth twitched at the corners as he spoke. "We've found a prohibited substance on these premises."

Susan screamed he was lying. I took the small plastic bag from Owens and looked at it.

"We'll soon settle this, Susan," I smiled. "Put junior down and roll up your sleeves."

Owens looked worried now. I tasted the contents of the bag. Heroin, and fairly pure stuff. Too pure for a user. And no pusher would sell it with that rate of purity. It needed cutting at least once more and even then would only be offered to advanced users.

Susan held out her arms. The skin was soft and unmarked. No tell-tale needle scars. I found some sweets in my pocket and gave one to the curly-headed kid.

"Susan, you go and pack some things for you and curly top. A short break with some friendly people will do you good. No panic. Everything under control now. You could save my life with a cup of coffee, though. Black, one sugar. None for this creep."

Susan closed the door behind her. I surveyed the mess Owens had made. A photo of the child lay on the floor, glass broken. Treasured ornaments lay in pieces. Deliberate vandalism. I smiled at Owens and hit him hard in the solar plexus. He doubled up, winded. I could smell the beer on his breath. I dragged him up by his hair and threw him into an armchair.

"Now then, son. Any time you'd like to continue this discussion I shall be overjoyed."

My voice was calm but inside I was angry. I wanted him to take a swing at me because then I could spread his nose all over his smug face and kick the rest of him into the shape of a soggy beanbag. He looked up with watery eyes and unsteady hands clamped on the arms of the chair. Not enough, I wanted him legless with fear.

"You dreary little small-town bully. Smashing up a kid's things is about your level. Stand up."

His hands went up to protect his head. I took his handcuffs out of his jacket and put them on him. Then I blindfolded him and told him to keep his mouth shut.

Barrett's men arrived. Both were big, discreet and efficient. Owens was taken outside and put in a Land Rover which drove away. Susan's cases were taken to the second vehicle. One of the escorts liked kids and was telling Susan's curly-topped daughter the story of Cinderella. I reckoned Little Red Riding Hood was more appropriate. Halloran had nabbed a big bad wolf.

Susan handed me the coffee. I offered her a cigarillo and she took it with as much enthusiasm as the Trojans had for the horse when they first saw it.

"You knew this would happen, you let it happen," she accused me. "They wreck my place and terrify my child and you let it happen."

"Yes."

"You frighten me, you know that? You scare me more than they did."

"I scare everyone. I'm good at it. Sorry about the house."

"I know it's not much. It's all I can afford since Julie's father left. Two years ago now. But we've managed. We don't ask for much. Then you come asking questions and they come threatening to take Julie into care and . . . "

Susan started to cry. The big blue eyes were full of confusion. Her make-up had run and underneath the superficial exterior of what I had at first thought was a high-octane performer when I first saw her was just a frightened, lonely girl. I put an arm around her and she started clinging. I looked around the tiny room at the damage and the wanton mess. I wondered how many other people received the same treatment around there. Okay, boys, you are first-rate at roughing up the defenceless. Now come and play with Halloran and see how you come off up against him.

Chapter 14

BARRETT LOOKED AT his office wall clock which showed 2.15 am. His round face creased into a frown. He tapped his pipe on the edge of the waste-paper basket and a flurry of fine ash descended.

"I could get the sack for this," he objected. "No, I could go inside for it."

"You just get back to your house and use your avuncular charm on the girl to prise a statement out of her. Then you keep her and the child under wraps for a few days so the Gwyns can't find them."

"Halloran, you're all heart. What about kidnapping a police officer?"

"What police officer? I lifted that little turd. He's blindfolded, alone and doesn't know where the hell he is or who has got him. Stop worrying, Barrett. I won't kill him if that's what you're thinking."

"I knew you were trouble the first time I saw you."

"Just get that statement from the girl. Leave it at the gatehouse. And give me your office keys. I'll hand them in on the way out."

"You're walking on thin ice," he warned. "You're a clever bastard all right and you know every trick in the book. But I don't like you. You'd blackmail the Pope if he had something you wanted, and fit him up so you could do it."

Barrett was a very fair judge of character.

*

Owens had been put in one of the old bomb-proof bunkers, handcuffed to a chair with his blindfold securely in place. Barrett had found an old canteen table which I had put six feet away from the chair. On the table was a glass of water, a pad of lined foolscap paper and two ball point pens.

The bunker smelled stale, dank and unused. Ideal for Owens to find himself in when the blindfold came off. The next thing he saw would be a shirtsleeved Halloran with white shirt criss-crossed with straps from the shoulder rig that held the forty-one Magnum. The combination should have been about right.

He blinked as I tugged the blindfold off. After a few seconds he realized what was around him and he was scared. The way I read him was the way he turned out to be, a young fool who had got sucked in to do the leg work for Ellis.

"Don't open your mouth, sonny. Just listen. Jack Lane was working for a secret government department, the same one I work for. We want to know exactly what happened. On the desk in front of you is writing equipment. Begin when I say go and keep on writing until I know all about it. Failure to comply will result in a fatal accident the details of which have already been prepared for Press release. A good effort may be rewarded by someone telling the Director of Public Prosecutions you were working on our behalf. Do you understand?"

Hell. I scare myself sometimes. It worked with Owens, and it worked because of the place I had put him in. Had I gone up to him on the street with a gun in his back and told him the same story he would have thought I was some kind of fruitcake. But in that cold, lonely bunker, at the mad Halloran's tea party, the familiar outside world did not exist.

We did not finish until 5.34 am. He knew nothing about Jack Lane's death, didn't know anyone who had a Browning, but did confirm that the complaints against me had been fabricated. No record of my arrest or detention existed. I knew that. Both he and Ellis had refrained from calling each other by name. No-one had checked in my personal belongings nor had they sealed or signed the envelope before giving those belongings back to me. He strenuously denied any knowledge of the bomb planted in my car and swore that Ellis would draw the line at killing. He knew Ellis intended to work me over but had no idea who the second man was. I believed him because there was a look in his eyes which told me that taking money to fit up or lean on suspects was one thing but permanent injury or physically killing anyone was another league altogether. He confirmed that Daniels had probably been in on the frame they had fitted me into.

I pocketed his statement and told him to get his family out of town for a few days and try not to talk to Daniels. If he had to justify his failure to silence the girl he was at liberty to tell Daniels everything I had told him. Then I borrowed the Land Rover and drove him, cuffed and blindfolded, ten miles north of the Llanmartin base. Dawn was beginning to break as I left him in a field by the side of a minor road with a herd of curious cows for company. He was a mile from the nearest village. How he freed himself was his problem. I left the handcuff key in his jacket pocket but didn't bother to tell him. Halloran's little initiative test.

I returned to the Llanmartin base and took photocopies of the statements made by Islwyn Evans, Susan and Owens. The originals I addressed to a quiet, even-handed but thorough and shrewd solicitor I knew. One set of copies I sent to Lucinda Bellamy. The others I retained. Although the statements were not properly attested or witnessed by anyone other than myself, they ought to convince Superintendent J. C. Daniels that he was dealing with someone who could play games as well or even better than he could.

I took breakfast at a sprawling transport café where the bacon was greasy, the sausages undercooked, the fried eggs hard and the mushrooms shrivelled. The great British breakfast with fried bread like hard tack and served with the courtesy and smiling face we have all come to know and love. But the tea was good and stewed, just the way I liked it. When you eat in the places I sometimes have to, be thankful for small mercies.

Omega section research had been busy that morning which I now realized was yesterday while I hung on to that outside line in the private room at the Oxford nick. I had addresses for the two jokers who had given evidence at the inquest on Natasha Madsen, Stuart Jacobs and the business consultant Kelly. Consulting the data banks from the D.H.S.S., the D.V.L.C., the Inland Revenue, the Public Records Office and the Lord Chancellor's Department, research had come up with the goods. Privacy in the computer age? No such thing.

At 10.09 am the sea breeze was knifing through my jacket. Below me, the resort of Jenkin's Quay nestled around the harbour, its houses terraced into ascending cliffs. I looked out over a grey, threatening sea that sprayed rollers against the harbour wall. The boats rode at anchor, rising and falling on the swell. Behind me, along the clifftop, the caravans stood like rows of squat sentinels peering anxiously down on the village below.

The caretaker pointed to Stuart Jacobs' caravan. Huddled into his black overcoat, eyes blinking rapidly, pink hands waving about, he reminded me of a mole whose hibernation I had prematurely disturbed. Needless to say he had not seen anyone for weeks. It was the off-season. The rent was paid to the office in Birmingham. Jacobs kept himself to himself.

I left the caretaker to his disturbed sleep and parked the Volvo as close as I could drive on the concrete road to Jacobs' caravan. Its thin curtains were drawn together. Every other van was deserted. I could see why. The breeze was not just healthy sea air but a soul-chilling wind that stung my face and brought tears to my eyes.

A crate of empty beer bottles stood outside the caravan door. The local rodents had been chewing the black plastic bag that spilled domestic rubbish over the grass. My knock sounded hollow. The wind blew in my ears and my head ached. I knocked again.

I tried the door handle. As I opened the door the smell hit me. I knew that smell. The gut-wrenching rotten smell of death. Mingled in with that stench was the odour of stale marijuana and cat's urine. I lit a cigarillo and propped the door open.

Inside, the caravan was a proper mess. The sink was full of congealed washing-up water, pan handles sticking out at crazy angles. The partition to the sleeping area was closed most of the way across. I wrestled with it for a while and managed to pull it mostly open.

Jacobs was face down on an unmade bed that stank of vomit. The vest he wore was stained yellow and the tatty denims were faded and dirty. He was cold and stiff as I rolled him over on to his back. A hypodermic lay on the bed beneath him. A hollow rubber tube was still in place on his left forearm. His flesh was the colour of white paper and the needle scabs on his arms were black. Glazed eyes stared at me disconcertingly. I let go of his arm and it flopped back lifelessly to join the rest of him. I pressed my fingers to the side of his neck and felt only cold, stiff meat. He had been dead for days.

I opened the windows to get some air in the place. I was wearing gloves so there were no problems about fingerprints. I started to go through his possessions, such as they were. Half an hour yielded little of interest. According to a crumpled letter behind the bed, Jacobs was a student who had failed his exams six months before. Now he had failed in the business of life. The dead twenty-year-old face stared at me but I could not tell him why.

The remnants of his last fix were in a small manila envelope on the floor. Something about the place was not right. There were no books or papers, driving licences or cheque books, letters from friends or the Social Security people, medical cards or even pieces of paper that he had scribbled his own private thoughts on. I tasted the contents of the envelope. Heroin. Pure heroin.

By the time it gets down to user level heroin has been adulterated or cut to about five per cent original purity by the addition of similar looking substances — mannite, quinine or lactose. An addictive drug, it eventually kills its victims within five years because it is a poison. But injected in its pure state, one fix is as instantaneously lethal as arsenic or strychnine. So who had given Stuart a lethal dose? Whether they had forced it on him or conned him into taking it, the end result was the same. Murder.

Maybe when they killed Jack they tidied up on the witnesses he had talked to. They obviously did not want to run the risk that Stuart would talk to anyone else.

Kelly's flat was in one of the old Victorian middle-class terraces at the residential end of Glyntywyn. The landlady was well into middle age, with a low centre of gravity, grey-rinsed hair and inquisitive eyes.

What a shame I had just missed Mr Kelly. He had left on a business trip the previous afternoon and she did not know when he would be back. Nothing unusual in that. He often came and went on business trips. He was a business consultant who travelled a lot. A polite man, he kept himself apart from everyone else but he was respectable. Not like the average Irishman that she would not have anything to do with.

The landlady was going to be a problem, I could tell. No, Mr Kelly had the only key to his room. Who was I? A policeman. I didn't look like a policeman. Why wasn't I in uniform and where were the local boys that she knew?

I wasted ten minutes while she made a cup of anaemic tea and I explained that it was a very confidential matter. Mr Kelly was suspected of a massive international fraud that swindled little old ladies and others out of their savings. Had she invested any money with him? Well, that was a relief. She would never have believed it of him.

A good operator could always earn a living as a con man. Always give the most plausible story to suit the individual circumstances. It saves bullying and beating the witnesses which invariably gets you noticed. Within five more minutes I was alone and celluloiding my way into Kelly's abode.

A business consultant should have business documents, or at least the odd copy of the Finance Act or *Accountancy Today* lurking around the place. Kelly had nothing of the sort. According to his landlady he worked from his rooms. So where was it all? A few raunchy paperbacks, a pack of cigarettes and some tinned food were all that remained to tell me about Kelly.

Except for the wardrobe which contained a pair of climbing boots beneath a pile of polythene bags the cleaners always put over your suits. At a guess I would have said that Kelly left in a hurry and missed those boots. Even a pro makes the odd mistake. Kelly was definitely a pro. He had sanitized the place clean.

I looked again at the paperbacks, the cigarettes and the tinned food. The tinned food was all high protein stuff. Survival rations. The paperbacks were the sort I read, fast-moving hard adventure fiction full of sex and impossible assignments — I like to see what I'm missing out on. The cigarettes were Gold Flake. You don't see those much these days. Export Brand. Kelly seemed like a travelling man. Maybe even in my line of work.

I parked the Volvo well out of sight of Divisional Police Headquarters in Glyntywyn. Give coppers a chance to remember a registration plate and they have access to all sorts of ancillary information. The difficult part of the operation was about to start, trying to convince Daniels that he should rat on Ives.

The way I imagined Daniels he was not the type you could physically bully. I would have to convince him that I was a swift-thinking, evil-minded bastard who had outmanoeuvred him. Had I outmanoeuvred him? Yes. Elizabeth said Daniels resented Ives because Ives knew too much. Remove the hold Ives had over Daniels and he would play. Yes, I was getting there slowly.

The desk boys were having a slow day, contemplating their end-of-shift brew. They ignored my arrival. You expect that sort of treatment at the post office but lethargy at the nick is disconcerting.

"Tell Daniels that Halloran wants him," I snapped.

The desk sergeant, more of a fixture than even his surroundings, picked up an intercom and spoke Welsh. Three minutes later I was in the presence.

I kept my coat on, even though the office temperature was at least twenty-two Centigrade. I had a good reason.

An iron man, Daniels, looking like you would expect an old-fashioned copper to look. Early fifties, five-ten and fifteen stone of muscle. His hands were hard, big and heavy, a boxer's hands. The accent was Rhondda and the square face hewn from an anthracite seam; a once broken nose had been re-set slightly off line. I could read Daniels' philosophy in his pale-blue eyes. A man who believed in the values of property, the law according to his own interpretation, and the abolition of the Judges' Rules.

"Sit down, Mr Halloran," he invited coldly. The emphasis was on the 'mister.'

So Daniels had been doing some checking. I guessed young Delme Owens had reported back.

"Do you know of any reason why I shouldn't lock you up for impersonating a police officer, kidnapping one of my men and assaulting him?" he demanded.

"That stupid you're not. Slow enough to let you be, I'm not. If I fail to call a friend every so often the information I already possess will be forwarded to the Home Office. That means that your Chief Constable, Special Branch, MI5, old Uncle Tom Cobbleigh and all bounce you and go through your books, paperwork, procedures and personnel like Torquemada and his bloody Inquisition. You're moderately bright, Daniels, but up against me in games of this sort, you're a babe in arms."

His heavy hands played with a coked-up briar pipe. Leaning his massive frame back in his leather swivel chair he looked intently at me. His blue eyes tried to pierce my brain to read what I knew.

"So what can I do for you?" he asked.

"You checked me out. What did you discover?"

He thought about whether he should tell me. If Daniels had a nickname it was probably Fox.

"You used to work for the government until recently. One of those departments in the Ministry of Defence that never advertise for personnel."

"Correct, or as nearly correct as you're likely to get. The late John Roderick Lane, known to his friends as Jack, was a mate of mine. Somebody killed him. The facts were covered up."

"So you say," Daniels countered. "So why hasn't there been an official investigation?"

Clever man. A fisherman in his spare time, maybe.

"I don't know. But I do know that I'm going to find his killer. And I'll do it with your help."

He chuckled. I didn't let it bother me. He had nothing in his hand. He was trying to bluff.

"Let's see if you find this amusing. I was fitted up the other evening by Elizabeth Gwyn and Adamson from the Lion. Two of your lads brought me to the nick, broke all the wrong rules and later, one of them, Ieuan Ellis, in company with A. N. Other worked me over something rotten and pistol-whipped me with a Browning automatic that looked remarkably like Jack Lane's. My car was left outside. Some lovely bastard put a bomb in it. I found the bomb. I have a corroborative statement for some of that from one of your men."

"Would that be D. C. Owens?"

"I also have two other statements that make interesting reading. One says that Jack Lane checked out of the Lion Hotel on Tuesday January the fourteenth and not on the sixteenth according to your report. That witness was threatened last night by Owens who tried to plant some heroin on her. Have a happy read."

I gave him the copy of Susan's statement.

"The original is in a place it would take you three lifetimes to find," I grinned.

Daniels laid the statement on his desk.

"In case you're thinking of sending someone round to her again, don't bother. She is under wraps."

Daniels smiled at me.

"I assume you want something in return for your silence about these ludicrous allegations."

He caught on fast.

"I want William Ives delivered to me, together with the evidence that he killed Jack Lane, namely a Browning GP35 automatic. I also want a man named Kelly. I want to talk to Ieuan Ellis. In return I keep my mouth shut about your misdemeanours and the corrupt activities of your family circle."

"What makes you think Ives had anything to do with it?"

"Natasha Madsen fell off a balcony during a party at Jenkin's Quay. The two witnesses who appeared were Kelly and Stuart Jacobs. Jacobs is dead. Heroin overdose. Someone wanted him out of the way. That someone was Ives. He didn't want it known he'd been at the party."

Daniels' eyes flickered for a second when I mentioned Stuart Jacobs' death. The news came as something of a shock to him. He reached in his uniform tunic pocket and produced a packet of cigarettes. He inhaled deeply. His blue eyes stared into mine which stared back. He was thinking very quickly about the best way to deal with me. I could almost see him take each option then reject it again.

"Give me one hour," he said. "Then meet me at Alan Gwyn's house. I'm sure that between us we can work something out."

"Fine. But don't get all excitable and spring any surprises. You'll be the first one I kill."

The anthracite seam cracked into a yawning gap of a very broad smile.

"I would not dream of it," he replied.

No-one followed me from the nick. I spent the next hour wandering around the shops and reloading the miniature transistorized recording device that I had kept hidden in my overcoat pocket during my conversation with Daniels. I addressed the cassette to my solicitor and posted it, recorded delivery at the main post office. I had to wait longer there than in the nick for some service. Needless to say I gave a false name and address of sender.

I hired a taxi for the afternoon. The driver was the talkative sort. When I told him where I was going, he shut up and drove. A five-mile journey gave me the chance to think. I reckoned Daniels might pretend to do a deal. The next stage of the operation was the play-it-by-instinct phase.

Chapter 15

THE GWYN RESIDENCE was a rambling red stone mansion set on a hill overlooking the broad sweep of the river. The long, tree-lined driveway had recently been re-surfaced. I was not the only visitor. A De Lorean sports car and an Audi Quattro had got there before me.

The grounds were extensive. Close-cropped lawns edged by well-tended flower beds and horse-chestnut trees. The house was freshly painted, the tarmac recent. One maintenance contract they had not skimped on. I was five yards from the door when a gun went off.

I had the Magnum in my hand before I hit the ground, rolling to the base of the nearest wall. Then a metallic noise sounded faintly and two more shots, loud and booming. Shotgun. But no lead came whistling my way. Whoever it was doing the shooting was not firing in my direction. That metallic noise again and a single shot. I picked myself up and felt foolish. Halloran paranoia. Don't judge everyone by your standards. Perhaps they won't try to kill you. That metal sound was a clay pigeon trap. Someone was shooting clays, behind the house.

I picked grit out of the palm of my left hand and breathed out deeply, counted to five for the tension to ease, and rang the doorbell, one of the old-fashioned type that pulled out from a recess in the wall. The au pair answered the door.

I always meet the really plain ones. This one was not even plain. More like downright ugly. Built like a Danish trawler, she had a mouth as wide as a wheelhouse door and her hands were like dead seals' flippers. I was expected, she told me, her voice sounding marginally less musical than a grindstone.

No expense had been spared on this modest dwelling. The living area I found myself in was bigger than a south-facing football pitch with a huge stone and copper chimney breast taking up the space where one set of goalposts would have been. The stone walls were hung with original oils depicting nineteenth-century rural splendours and the cocktail cabinet was like a small bar.

I walked through easy-opening French windows on to a large patio. Daniels and Alan Gwyn were together at the far end, sitting by a clay pigeon trap. A third man, dark hair curling over the collar of a skeet vest, stood some yards away ready to take the next clays.

"Pull," he shouted.

The trap's arm sprung forward faster than the eye could follow. The clays, two bakelite discs, flashed into the air towards a line of fir trees. I watched the shooter. Smooth, flowing action as his gun came easily to the shoulder and the muzzles swung through the first target. He fired once, still swinging and fired again. Both clays were powdered into tiny fragments. Useful shooting.

He turned and smiled at me, broke the gun, a twelve gauge over and under. The spent cartridge cases were ejected crisply, smoke wisping after them. He rested the gun muzzle on his toe and removed the ear muffs he wore.

"Mr Halloran is here," he announced to his two companions, then turning to me again: "I'm Garth Gwyn."

"Useful shooting," I observed.

He was taller than Alan Gwyn and thinner but I could not mistake the facial resemblance. More of an athlete, he was at least ten years younger than his brother and there was something of the young playboy who had not quite grown up about him. More polished of manner, he was nonetheless more aggressive, yet in a more cultured way.

The smile became an intense and unfriendly stare. He casually dropped two cartridges into the breech of the gun from a cartridge box attached to his leather belt.

"And you?" he asked coldly. The meaning was clear. He was issuing a challenge.

For a second or two I thought he might try something silly. A holstered handgun should never beat a loaded shotgun but he had to close the breech, level and fire the weapon. All I had to do was draw. Which gave me an edge. And I had killed men. This trick-shooting youngster hadn't. He might be a good clay shot, because that is trick shooting no matter what anyone tells you. But he would be no match for me. I always regarded an opponent as just another hostile target — never a human being.

"Don't try me," I warned.

"Good advice," Daniels confirmed. "Don't be stupid, Garth."

Garth Gwyn smiled again.

"Sorry, brother-in-law. Just thought it might solve your problems."

He withdrew the two cartridges and started clearing up his equipment. Daniels' sound advice had prevailed and Alan Gwyn had found the exercise interesting. We went inside and Alan Gwyn said:

"John here is advising an accommodation with you. What guarantees can you give?"

"I didn't kill your idiot brother out there. I'm only homicidal with good reason. By the way, where is Mrs Gwyn?"

He looked angrily at me. The deep-set hazel eyes were wild and his heavy face reddened. I had said the wrong thing. I wondered why.

"My wife no longer lives here. I will be divorcing her."

Daniels cut in with:

"It seems Elizabeth and Mr Ives have gone away together. Alan is rather upset by developments. I'll explain to you outside."

My heart did not exactly bleed for him.

Dusk was gathering as Daniels and I talked together in front of the house. He gave me the impression that he was resigned to dealing with me.

"Ives was responsible for Lane's death. I covered up for him because he had information that could land me and Alan in prison. Elizabeth left last night and I presume Ives has gone with her. He is not at the base. He and Elizabeth have been carrying on for some time. Kelly has also left the area. He may be tied up with Ives."

"Ieuan Ellis?"

"Resigned the day after he worked you over. Said he had another job. Haven't seen him since."

"Very convenient for you."

"I'm giving you what you asked for."

"Where is Elizabeth now?"

"Took the evening flight to Zurich. She has money in Switzerland. Here's the flight number. Find her and I reckon you'll find Ives."

Daniels handed me a piece of paper. Our eyes met and neither of us smiled. Then he asked:

"Why do you think Kelly killed that inquest witness Jacobs and then disappeared?"

"I really have no idea," I replied.

"Why did you go and see him?"

This Daniels was a shrewd man. He did not really believe that my sole motive was to nail Ives for Jack's killing. He suspected I wanted to know about Natasha Madsen's death, which I did. Because it had been bothering me. So I gave him an evasive answer, and one which was only half-true.

"Because I thought he might let on that you rigged another inquest verdict. More leverage for me in my dealings with you."

"Why pick on that inquest?" he insisted.

"Jack liked young girls," I lied. "She was a former sleeping partner in previous holiday arrangements."

He lit a cigarette and the pale-blue eyes bored into me.

"You will stick to our arrangement?"

"If you have stuck to yours. And it seems like you have."

"I have. You ought to be able to find Ives in Zurich."

Daniels watched me walk down the drive. With his crooked brain he was wasted out here. He could have made a fortune in the Met.

I drove back to London through darkness and driving rain. I did not trust Daniels and the Gwyns. They might have kept their part of the bargain but I was sure they had told Ives I wanted him. Which did not make me feel so bad about breaking my end of the deal. Because when I had Ives I would be presenting all the evidence I had on Daniels and the Gwyns to Sir Simon Verity. He could then pass it on to the other part of the Home Office which dealt with such civil matters.

As yet I had no idea what Ives looked like. And if you are chasing a target it is a good idea to know what you are looking for. I hid the Volvo in a discreet lock-up garage I used under another identity and arrived by taxi at the Alamo just after ten.

Sean was on the dance floor with a teenage heiress entwined round him. I sent the gay waiter over with a message. Sean looked over his shoulder, noticed me, and gave the adoring sylph to a chinless wonder.

We went through to Sean's private office. He closed the door, leaned on it and breathed out heavily. Then he raised his eyes to heaven as if in silent prayer.

"Thank God no-one was watching for you."

"Meaning?" I asked.

"They are after you and they mean business."

Butterflies started dancing in my stomach. Sean does not joke about the serious things in life. If he said someone was after me, I had to take notice.

"Who?" I asked.

"Two executive types. One is from the Embassy. Harman S. Talbot the Third. Ivy League person. Legal cover for the N.S.A. at Grosvenor Square. Someone snitched about me asking for the happy snap of Ives. Strange thing, though, Harman mentioned you by name. He was round about seven this evening with a message. You are retired. Don't meddle in what does not concern you or you won't be around any more to get concerned. A diplomat, Harman. The look in his eye said they'd wipe you out without a second thought."

I took the photo Sean handed me and put it in my wallet.

"Thanks, mate. I owe you. If they visit again, say you passed on the message and I'm no longer your friend."

Sean was about to give me some good advice. I got in first.

"And tell Harman S. Talbot the Third that I said if he does try anything he'll be Harman S. Talbot the Last."

Sean suppressed a grin and returned to his teenage heiress. I went out the back way and stepped very carefully out into the street.

The game plan was clear. Ives knew I was after him so he had called out the cavalry to protect himself. The scenario would have gone something like this. Ives contacted his superiors who diplomatically enquired as to who I was. The answer they got probably encouraged them to think I was a lunatic now off the official strength and therefore solely responsible for my own actions. Mowlam would have planted that information in such a way that it would get through to the N.S.A. brass. They would then take a decision regarding my future. I no longer enjoyed the protection of my service so I was fair game. Remember, agents almost never kill each other. Repercussions are too heavy.

No-one followed me as I walked by the river. The lights of the city were reflected in the water. The reflections reminded me of an old saying of Jack Lane's. 'In the Hall of Mirrors, each set of facts is capable of two interpretations. One innocent, the other sinister.

Test each set of facts both ways, Halloran. That way you might see what everyone else is playing at. It might just keep you alive in a tight corner.'

I flicked my cigarillo butt into the water and a shower of sparks fell and died out. Sitting on that old bollard I did some hard thinking trying to make sense out of it all.

The Gwyns were an ancillary problem. Like Jack Lane and myself they were players in the game, used by Ives either willingly or unwillingly. And he was still using them to report on my movements and to tell me what he wanted me to know. The main problem was Ives, together with everyone else who was sticking their nose into my vendetta against Jack's killer. I tried to tell myself I was being dispassionate about it all, just wanting to see a job through. But I had to be honest with myself. I wanted to kill someone in return for Jack.

I could not work out Bo Pepper's motive for not squashing me in that motorway sandwich before flavouring me with 9mm Parabellum. Bo and I went back a long time but business was business with Bo. If I was on the list, I would be gathered. So why had he shown his hand and deliberately pulled back?

Answer. Bo was warning me what might happen to me. And showing me how vulnerable I was.

Next question. Why had Harman S. Talbot the Third stuck his warning in? Why warn me? Why not just do it? Now I had to get this answer right. Wrong would be fatal.

Answer. The N.S.A. wanted to be seen issuing a warning. Seen by whom, the British, or Ives?

I reckoned the best bet was Ives.

Something had been bothering me about this whole business, ever since I discovered Natasha Madsen was Verity's stepdaughter and a C.I.A. operative. The Company must have known of her relationship to Verity. Her inexperience was obvious. Yet they had sent her down to Glyntywyn with a cover that was ludicrously dangerous and when she failed to come back, the Deputy Director from Langley who sent her in the first place forbade London Station C.I.A. to investigate. Why?

Answer. Either C.I.A. were trying to start a war with their

colleagues in N.S.A. or they were trying to bring Ives to someone's attention. Verity's. Had to be. Why else use his stepdaughter? Therefore Ives was up to something against his own side's interests. What could that be?

Either he had sold out to the other side or they wanted someone else to take him off their hands. Crazy idea. I lit another cigarillo to ease the strain of my private brainstorming session.

The temptation to sound out my ideas on Verity was considerable. But my instincts told me to play it close. Verity and Mowlam wanted me to go after Ives. I suspected Ives wanted me to go after Ives. So that's where I would go, to Zurich. But first I had to see Lucinda Bellamy.

Chapter 16

I ARRIVED ON Lucinda's doorstep at 11.40 pm, suitcase in hand.

"You look like an evacuee," she laughed.

"You're not old enough to have seen one and I'm certainly not old enough to have been one. Let me in. I feel vulnerable out here."

I was tired and hungry and feeling the strain. Lack of sleep and living on my nerve ends down in Glyntywyn were beginning to dull my survival instincts. I didn't want to go back to my flat in case Harman S. Talbot's warning might be for real or Ives had some private enterprise waiting for me. If they knew Sean was a friend of mine, they knew where I lived. And I had enough enemies in the Security and Intelligence establishments who would pass on any information about me at the drop of a hat. An Omega Section man made a lot of enemies over the years.

"You look all in. I'll cook you something. Pour yourself a drink."

"Thanks but I'd rather have some strong coffee."

I lay on the sofa for a while and closed my eyes. I was just drifting off when the telephone rang. Lucinda answered and held out the receiver.

"For you, darling. Someone called Gunther."

He was his usual cheery self. I had called him from the Blue Bell on my way through Brecon earlier in the day.

"Elizabeth Gwyn is in Zurich. She is with two men named Ives and Kelly. My boys are freezing their fingers off keeping observation. I've booked you on the flight arriving at Berne four am. Be on it. You owe me a long explanation."

Gunther hung up on me before I had the chance to hang up on him. Tomorrow would be fun. Gunther was a Calvinist. And Calvinists don't seem to have a sense of humour, especially on Sundays.

I didn't get the chance to lie down again. Lucinda brought in a Spanish omelette. She had obviously never done the cordon bleu course.

"I should have warned you. I can't cook."

"You said it. Then you can't be good at everything can you?"

She laughed, wickedly, and poured me some more coffee. It's hard to ruin coffee.

"According to my employer, you're supposed to be reporting progress."

"I work alone and keep my thoughts to myself until I have something concrete to say. There is a written report on its way to you via the G.P.O."

"That's breach of standard procedures," she objected.

"So no-one will think of intercepting it, will they?"

She looked sideways at me and sat pensively, long legs tucked underneath her on the sofa. She really was a striking-looking girl. If ever I married, I would marry someone who looked like her.

"What are you thinking, H?" she asked.

"How I'm going to stay alive for the next few days. Your employer is a devious character, you know."

"I'm impressed by his ability."

"Bully for him."

"You're not jealous, are you?" she teased.

"An emotion not felt by the Halloran. I'm on to Ives."

She was excited about that.

"Where is he?"

"In Switzerland. Call me a cab to take me to the airport, will you. I'm due in Zurich at earliest availability."

She lit a cigarette and dialled the minicab service. I finished the omelette and chased the taste away with coffee.

"On its way. You look worried. Ives is on to you, is he?"

"The N.S.A. have been making threatening noises. It could be a trap."

"Do be careful, H. I want you back in one piece."

The way she kissed me told me she meant what she said.

I almost missed the plane, one of those short-haul jets you can never sleep on. I hate flying because aircraft worry me. It's a long way down from twenty thousand plus feet without a parachute. I never minded flying in the Army because I always had a parachute. I started off as one of those idiots that jumped out of planes. Our glorious forebears were the guys who went a bridge too far at Arnhem. Our successors were the lads who pulled the politicians' fat out of the fire at Goose Green and Longdon. In my day all you had to worry about as far as the aircraft were concerned was being mangled up in the tailplane if you didn't clear the slipstream.

As a passenger, I was easily bored. I could never get into reading a book. On the longer-haul flights, the movies seem repetitive. And I've yet to score with one of those uniformed sets of flashing teeth set in a colour-supplement face. They know more hand-offs, verbal and physical, than a London Welsh three-quarter.

Airport Security at Zurich were bored. At that early hour of the morning even the terrorists and urban guerrillas were in bed. The Customs gave me one of those unspoken looks they always give people like me at airports. They did not ask me to open my case but waved me through as if it was all too much bother to do anything else. I knew why. A dark-overcoated man with the demeanour and bearing of an undertaker had thrown them a warning look from his vantage point in a doorway before vanishing into a knot of travellers.

I went to look for a taxi. As I passed through a reception hallway I had my eyes peeled for watchers. There shouldn't have been any because Gunther had deliberately given my wrong arrival point as Berne over the the telephone. Just in case anyone was tapping Lucinda's phone. Rigby of Internal Security had never lied to me in fifteen years. And he said his Minister had ordered him to watch her.

But there was a look-out. He was standing by the news-stand, flicking through a copy of *Paris Match*, his briefcase near his well-polished shoes. Not local talent but an off-base import. No-one resident in Zurich in January wore lightweight suits covered by light mackintoshes. No. This one had to be Ives' watcher, hastily despatched to keep an eye on this incoming flight.

There was another look-out drinking coffee in a lounge area. This one was local talent, judging by the ski-pants and fur jacket. Female, late thirties, she had back-up; a ski-instructor type, blond hair on top of chunky Germanic features who was covering one exit from the comfort of a bar recess.

The tandem watchers did not move as I passed through. But when the business executive type with his now-folded *Paris Match* tailed me through the exit, they moved in behind him.

From nowhere, a cab pulled to a halt in front of me. I thought it was a snatch and reached for the Magnum. The cab driver spoke German to me.

"Gunther is waiting."

I climbed in the back of the cab, a black Mercedes, and looked back towards the exit. The business executive type had fallen over the girl in ski-pants. Her hefty ski-instructor friend was helping them both up. But he was clumsy and only succeeded in falling over himself. The group was still entangled as my cab turned the corner and accelerated. I liked that driver. No ostentatious burning of the tyre rubber round squealing corners that would get us noticed, just a steadily increasing speed that distanced us quickly from the airport by making judicious use of the straight bits of road.

"Gunther knows you are here. He is waiting at base. Good flight from London?" the driver asked.

"About the same as any flight," I replied.

"Gunther is not happy," he warned me. "You know him long?"

"Too long."

"That is good."

. "Were those your people at the airport, the girl and the blond man who collided with my watcher?"

"No. They were C.I.A."

The Swiss do everything properly. Two maintenance men frisked me at the entrance to a windowless building that looked like a high-technology centre. The taller one handed the taxi-driver my Magnum and he tucked it in his waistband. He was already carrying my suitcase. I followed him down rubber-floored corridors to a lift. We descended two storeys to the depths of a soulless underworld where the fluorescent lighting hurt my eyes and no sound issued from behind the doors. Outside an office marked J17 we halted and my escort knocked on the door.

"Enter." The command was in German.

Gunther was seated at a desk, drinking coffee. Opposite him a line of television screens and a radio-control system were inordinately active considering the early hour. Pictures on the screens showed the exterior of the building we were in and several areas of street. I guessed the infra-red cameras were situated on all the streets for half a block around the building.

Gunther stood up. Everyone's idea of a Swiss bureaucrat, he was fifty, bespectacled and dour. The grey face was neutral of shape and almost devoid of character. His suit was the same. Behind the door hung a dark overcoat and Russian fur hat. The room was full of cigarette smoke. Uncharacteristically, Gunther smoked Gitanes incessantly.

His thick, nicotine-stained hand shook mine with a firmness that made me suspect he would rather be shaking me warmly by the throat. The pale-grey eyes were like burning lasers behind the thick spectacles.

"Give him his gun back, Otto."

"Airport. Three watchers. Two C.I.A. intercepted a third man," Otto reported and left the room.

A grey telephone on Gunther's desk buzzed alarmingly. He

listened intently for ten seconds and then said:

"I'll come up. Excuse me, Halloran. An operation has reached crisis point. I will return soon."

Gunther was too old a hand to let an outsider in on the secrets of an operation that was solely his proprietorial concern. I sipped my lonely cup of coffee and waited.

I had made many contacts over the fifteen years I had been in the game. Some were combative, out for what they could get, to enhance their own standing at your expense. Others co-operated unwillingly, because someone in a higher position had told them to give you a helping hand. The majority resented the fact that you were better than they were. They all traded favours with you, trying to make better use of you than you could of them. They varied in ability from brilliant through adequate to downright bloody incompetent, with most at the lower end of the ability scale. But a very few were real professionals who understood that ours was a rotten business and that we were all in the same leaky boat and that there were mutual advantages in playing it straight down the line. Out of this understanding, friendships occasionally grew. Perhaps not real friendships but the nearest you could get in our business.

Gunther came into this last category. We had worked together very successfully on several occasions. He was about the best I had seen. We trusted each other because we had to, both knowing that when the time came to look after our individual interests to the detriment of the other's we were both straight enough to give each other advance warning. But that didn't stop us from keeping each other up to the mark, using all the tricks of the trade and some that had not yet been classified.

I thought about sneaking a crafty look at all Gunther's paperwork. Then again there would be little point. Gunther would not have left it lying around if there was anything he didn't want me to see. After watching the television screens for a few moments I was getting bored. Then Gunther returned.

"My apologies, Halloran. The Romanians are up to something."

"Didn't know they were that well organized."

"They are not."

"So what's new? Where is Ives?"

"I take it this business concerns Natasha Madsen. I do like to have an official reason for committing so much manpower to one enquiry. It looks better than stating on a report that the official aim, as sanctioned by me, is helping out a retired colleague on a private matter. Our budgets are now strictly controlled. There is not the money around that there used to be."

The Swiss too. The Arabs would run out of oil next.

"You want an explanation?"

"Please. My boys are watching your target."

"Got any Scotch?"

"No."

I took out the duty free malt.

"A present from Scotland."

"Which you will proceed to drink. Thank you, Halloran."

Gunther poured two measures more accurately than an automatic dispenser would have dared.

"Prosit. To your retirement, H, old friend. Try and remain retired. The word around the woods is that the N.S.A. do not love you. Ives is N.S.A. So why should I help you?"

"Because I need your help, because we hacked two big ones last year and because you're nothing but a sentimental ex-copper who must have something to complain about."

"And because there is no-one else," Gunther added.

"Ives is N.S.A. Madsen died suspiciously on my ground while investigating him. Jack Lane died finding out what happened to Madsen. I want Ives back in the U.K. so I can talk to him. Do me a favour and put him on the next plane out with Elizabeth Gwyn and Kelly. I'll pick them up at Heathrow."

I had made my opening pitch. No way was Gunther going to agree but I had to start bargaining somewhere. This was his territory and I knew enough not to go starting anything without telling him. He was the sort to take offence if his friends didn't play by his rules.

"So you have stumbled on an inter-departmental American war. Your people want to make capital so they retire you officially and send you after Ives because you and Jack were old friends. H, unless you produce an official request I cannot do what you ask."

128

"I want Ives."

"My chief can already have my head for this. I have one entire team on Ives. I will have to take my people off. It is not a Swiss affair."

Gunther must have been slowing down in his old age. He never used to tell his chief anything.

"I understand. Neutrality and all that. Give me the location, back off and go back to guarding your industrial and financial secrets."

Gunther stretched fat legs beneath the desk. He had put on weight. Living off the brokerage of Europe and an easy life did that for him.

"Nor can I turn a blind eye while you arrange to snatch him. What's the plan? You sightsee while a team takes him?"

"I've seen enough gnomes and your architecture is grey. I'm on my own. There will be a fracas and someone will get hurt. But I want Ives."

"You know they are expecting you."

Not a question, a statement. I could see Gunther thinking about gunfire and innocent civilians in the way.

"Yes."

He banged his fist on the desk.

"You are a crazy man, Halloran. They arrive yesterday, or the day before now. They check into a hotel using their correct names and then move out to a house on the outskirts, leaving its address at the hotel so that even a child may follow them. They want you to find them. It is a trap. They have been leaving telegrams for you along the way."

"That's what I figured they would do."

I poured more Scotch while Gunther sat silently.

"Gunther. Just keep any outsiders off my back while I get into that house. I'll nab Ives. Keep the others in custody for a few hours until I get him away. You owe me. Remember?"

Gunther already knew what I was going to suggest.

"If in future I want the Crown Jewels you will make sure your former employers will give them to me," he warned.

"Done," I replied.

Gunther smiled. He knew he had been.

Chapter 17

GUNTHER DROVE SEDATELY, deliberate in his every movement. The grey eyes were alert to the movements and direction of all other traffic. And I could see by the fact that he kept one eye continually on the driving mirror that he had not lost any of his street skills.

The Peugeot was like Gunther — neat and very clean. It was the only car I had ever ridden in where the ashtrays were always empty and the interior always looked the way it did when the vehicle left the factory. Occasionally he spoke German into the radio and received reports from different sources. He had two other operations on the go as well as my problem. Yet he had the ability to compartmentalize it all in that card index of a mind.

We stopped behind a block of flats. The lift had to be the only one in Zurich not working. Gunther regarded the stairs distastefully. Annoyed, he spoke into a radio handset.

"Get that lift repaired when you leave."

"Yes, sir." The far-off reply was riddled with static.

By the tenth floor Gunther was wheezing breathlessly. A coded knock on a black door was answered by a stocky character in overalls. His colleague was watching from the window with an infra-red telescope mounted on a tripod. Next to it was a camera with long-range lens.

Like end-of-shift watchers the world over, these boys were tired, unshaven and full of convenience food. Gunther did not introduce me and they did not ask questions. My presence was accepted as a matter of routine.

The object of attention was a detached house at the end of a cul-de-sac, two hundred yards and a street away. Split level, the house was set back twenty yards from the roadway and the garden behind was walled. It was an executive residence, probably belonging to some upper-echelon manager. In its wide driveway was the inevitable Mercedes. The curtains were closed, only to be expected at five in the morning, and the surrounding area seemed quiet enough. The respectable burghers of the suburb were enjoying their well-earned rest.

Gunther tapped my shoulder as I used binoculars to familiarize myself with the layout. His chubby finger stabbed towards the open end of the cul-de-sac. An Audi was parked strategically, with one man apparently asleep at the wheel. We were not the only party interested in the house. Now who the hell was dozing in that Audi?

Gunther's assistant, the stocky one who was eating an open *Bierwurst* sandwich, handed over a sheet of paper. The Mercedes in the driveway was a hire car. The Audi was registered to a German firm of management consultants.

"C.I.A. front," the stocky man announced.

"Who's in the house?" I asked.

He spread out a number of photographs on the table, dealing them face down like an expert card player. On the back were written the names Elizabeth Gwyn, Liam Kelly and William Ives. I turned them face upwards, starting with Elizabeth Gwyn. She looked windswept and nervous. The photo of Liam Kelly showed a man in his early thirties, with close-cropped fair hair and the kind of rugged face that looked like it meant business. That face was vaguely familiar. It might just have been that I recognized it from the warehouse in Glyntywyn. But that wasn't the only time I had seen it, I was sure. But I had seen a lot of faces over the years and I could not place this one. So I turned over the photo of William Ives and it wasn't. I recognized that face clearly enough. It belonged to former Detective Sergeant Ieuan Ellis. Taking the photo of Ives that Sean had given me out of my wallet I laid it alongside Ellis's photo. Gunther looked askance at me.

"I've been had. Ives is not in that house."

I turned up two other unnamed photos and they were not Ives. Faces I had never seen before but they were known to Gunther.

"Local talent. Sitters. Hired for the occasion," he informed me.

"So now you know it really is a trap shall we pack up and go home?"

I shook my head.

"I still want to talk with them."

"Walk up to that front door and you will get your face blown off. The two sitters are killers. One or two good contracts around Europe to their names."

I lit a cigarillo and settled down in a chair.

"Who owns the house?" I asked.

"Local executive who is on holiday lives there. The house is owned by the Desmond Donoghue Delta Data Corporation."

"I won't ask you to say that again. American. So what do you know about it?"

"It is incorporated in Liechtenstein," Gunther replied.

That was all I would get on it. Liechtenstein rivalled the Swiss in the opaque society stakes. Set up a company in Vaduz and the only man who would ever know was the lawyer doing the paperwork. And he was not allowed by law to repeat the details, even to himself.

The name Donoghue rang some kind of bell in the back of my mind and I couldn't remember whether I had heard it in some professional context or not. It would need checking out. But Gunther was ahead of me.

"Wealthy American political power broker," he announced. "His industries make everything from cement to aspirins including electronics and some very sophisticated military hardware. Maybe Ives has gone private."

"Your researchers have been busy."

Gunther bowed stiffly in mock acknowledgement.

The dark hours became dawn then a crisp sunlight morning. At 9.28 am two men emerged from the house, one carrying a suitcase. Through the binoculars I could see Liam Kelly and Ellis. The ex-detective was hunched into a green anorak. Both men stood around for a while then Ellis started the Audi. Kelly noted his immediate surroundings, cars, the passers-by and the windows overlooking him. Seemingly satisfied, he joined Ellis in the Audi. They drove off in the direction of the city.

"Gunther. Have them followed," I instructed.

He looked at me as though I were some kind of excitable virgin.

"Four cars are on standby. That leaves the woman and two babysitters in the house."

"The C.I.A. are tailing them," the stocky watcher announced, rubbing his eyes.

With the odds halved I would never have a better chance. It was time to go in.

"I'll pay a visit, Gunther."

"It's still two to one," he warned.

I checked the loads in the forty-one Magnum. Gunther threw me a pair of overalls with the electricity company logo on the front.

"Van downstairs. Put those on. I'll go in the back way."

Gunther put the binoculars down and checked the magazine of his Sig P210 automatic pistol and slipped the gun into his overcoat pocket.

"It's my show," I announced.

He smiled.

"It was my show in Lucerne two years back. That didn't stop you saving my neck. You are a nuisance, Halloran, but I cannot see you walking into a trap. Karl, have the local police block that cul-de-sac. No vehicles to come in until I give the word."

The Volkswagen van really did belong to the electricity company. Gunther had given me a small radio transmitter receiver so we could stay in contact with each other. I waited until he confirmed he was in position then I drove towards the cul-de-sac. The first hundred yards I was on the left of the road and wondered why this idiot in a Citroën driving straight at me was sounding his horn. Steady, Halloran. You're in Switzerland now. They drive on the right, remember.

I cruised along the cul-de-sac with my stomach knotted up and my palms sticky with perspiration. With the toolbox in my left hand and the clipboard tucked under my right arm I walked up the short driveway to the house whistling happily. A good impersonation of an electricity man. I rang the front doorbell confidently and stood admiring the morning.

The door opened fractionally. I spoke German. There was a

fault in the area and we were checking the houses to find it. Could I come in?

The small Italian type was suspicious and he had shifty eyes that told me. He closed the door behind me as I looked for the junction box and stood watching as I lay the toolbox down. No way could I have left the Magnum in its shoulder holster because the overalls were too tightly buttoned to allow a fast draw. I had put it in the toolbox instead.

My problem was that I didn't know where the other man was. I wasn't kept in ignorance for long. He appeared on the stairway, a heavy Germanic type the width of a brick wall with no neck and unfriendly eyes.

They had rumbled me. Either that or they didn't like utility men. The Italian at the front door was fast on his feet and even faster with a flashing knife that missed me by an inch. I let go one shot that didn't and he was bowled over by the impact of a .41 wadcutter through his chest. I rolled and came up facing the man on the stairs.

This one was the gunfighter. The Luger in his left hand had a barrel as long as your arm. But his right hand slipped on the toggle action as he tried to feed a round up the spout. I gave him a chance.

"Freeze."

His decision only took him a split second and he decided the wrong way. The toggle was half back when I blew his head off. The impact of my second shot threw him sideways over the banisters. His exploding cranium had spattered a horrible mess all over the wallpaper and the stair carpet.

I rolled again and came up next to the dead knife-thrower. His right arm twitched but it was only a reflex action. Then I heard the back door go in and a woman started screaming. I ran through an open doorway, a large room, and took cover by the next doorway.

The woman was now swearing excitably in Welsh. She wanted Gunther to take his podgy hands off her.

"H, you okay?" he called out.

"Come ahead and bring that red-headed witch with you."

Elizabeth Gwyn was pushed through the open doorway. Gunther was not taking any chances.

She was half-dressed in a pair of men's pyjamas, the top half.

"Hello again," I said coldly, grabbing her arm and dragging her into the hallway.

She caught sight of the dead Italian and then the brain-stained wallpaper and carpet. Turning away from the scene in horror she clung on to me and started to retch. I dragged her back again into the room and threw her on to the sofa. Gunther holstered the Sig and lit a Gitanes. He could see I wanted a private discussion so he tactfully wandered off into the hallway.

Elizabeth was trembling like a frightened animal and staring at the floor. I lit a cigarillo and realized my hand was still shaking.

"Kelly and Ellis. Where are they?" I demanded.

"Ellis is coming back. He took Kelly to the airport," she whimpered.

"Where is Kelly going?"

"I don't know. Don't treat me like a criminal."

The green eyes were terrified. She reached for a pack of cigarettes on a small coffee table and failed to extract one. Her hands were still shaking too much. Mine were still shaking too, but in anger. This lynx had set me up in Glyntywyn, and now she was part of a similar ploy again. I noticed a housecoat lying on a chair and threw it at her.

"Okay. Put that on. My friend is a Calvinist. Legs as good as yours are considered sinful."

She shouted at me.

"Damn you. They were going to kill me, you fool. When they'd got you, I was next."

I yelled to Gunther to watch the road, that Ellis was coming back. Elizabeth looked plaintively at me.

"I had to trap you," she explained tearfully. "I didn't want any more of this."

Instead of putting the housecoat on, she took the pyjama top off and stood self-consciously, hands by her sides. Then she turned around slowly to show me her back. It would have been a beautiful back except that it was criss-crossed with red weals and scars that had cut into the flesh. What had not bled was badly bruised, a mottled purple-black bruising that extended to the backs of her thighs. She turned again to face me and I could see bruises on her stomach and upper arms.

"My husband did that to me," she cried. "I took you to your hotel room because he threatened to cut me on my breasts. He hadn't hurt my breasts yet, you see. He said he liked my breasts."

I put the housecoat round her and found some brandy. She gulped at it eagerly and took the cigarette I handed her. Now I'm a hardened character who'll break an opponent's ribs or blow his head off without worrying too much about the moral issues involved. But cold-blooded violence and disfiguration is a nutter's game. And to inflict gratuitous pain, especially on women, and enjoy doing it, means you ought to be in a very secure institution to stop you ever doing it again. A secure institution like a six-foot hole in the ground.

She was telling the truth, I reckoned. After all, the last words she said to me in that Glyntywyn hotel room were: "I'm sorry, I'm sorry."

"Tell me," I invited.

She shook her head.

"No way. And have this done to me again? Or have that lunatic Kelly set on me? I'm staying right here, in Switzerland, and I'm asking for police protection. I've got money here that Alan hid away over the years and I'm never going back."

"Sorry, Elizabeth. You have no choice. My Calvinist friend out there will put you on the next plane back to London where the police will be waiting for you. I will have told them about how you trapped me in the Lion Hotel and about how some of your friends rigged my car to explode. I'll also tell them about Jack Lane."

She screamed and threw the brandy glass at me, tried to gouge my eyes out and ruin my prospects of a continuing sex life. So I wrestled her down to the floor, straddled her and said simply.

"Tell me and my friend will arrange protection. Clam up and it's the next plane home."

There is an old saying which goes: 'Sometimes you have to be cruel to be kind.' I was being cruel, I felt cruel but it was the only way. She was a determined girl, frightened of her husband and what he could do yet willing to stand up to me. I had to convince

136

her that I was a bigger bastard than her husband without actually physically hurting her.

I picked her up, put her back on the sofa, and gave her another brandy.

"Throw that at me and I'll hurt you worse than Alan ever would. I want the facts. Then Gunther out there will provide the protection."

She started sulking because she knew I meant what I said. I left her to think about it for a minute or two while I went for a quiet word with Gunther. He was poking about in the recesses that interest ex-coppers like him when they are at a loose end for ten minutes. He agreed to my proposal that he protect Elizabeth if she came across with the goodies and only raised the ante to the freehold on M.I.5 records as consideration for his promise.

Elizabeth looked meekly at me when I went back in. She knew I had won. For me, there was no satisfaction in the victory.

She started with how Ives came to be involved with her husband. He had turned up in the Glyntywyn area with evidence of the Gwyns' corrupt misdeeds and an introduction from someone in the States who was supposedly a friend of Garth's from the days when the younger Gwyn had been at the Harvard Business School. The deal was that the Gwyns with Daniels' help provide a protective screen for the Whitesands Head Base and notify of any strangers in the area. Standard security practice. Natasha Madsen started snooping around and got herself noticed, involved herself in a relationship with Garth and died at the party. Ives had been there but didn't want it known. Stuart Jacobs, the heroin freak, and Liam Kelly gave evidence at the inquest to the effect there had been no drugs present at the party. Wrong. Garth liked the occasional snort of coke and there had been more acid floating around than in a commercial vehicle battery factory. Elizabeth didn't know but I guessed Ives had fed Natasha Madsen some acid and thrown her off the balcony. Kelly knew Ives and bribed Jacobs to give bent evidence.

Then Jack Lane came on the scene and picked Elizabeth up one night at the Willows while husband Alan was on business elsewhere. Both got what they wanted: Elizabeth some companionship from a kind man and Jack the information about the party. Then came the messy part, the whole bloody silly irony about the way Jack died.

Elizabeth returned home on the Tuesday morning early to find Alan had not gone away on business. He wanted to know where she had been. He beat it out of her. Being mindful of his position in the locality and not wanting to look stupid if everyone knew his wife was having it away with passing travellers, he sent Ellis and Kelly after Jack. Kelly was Ives' man, foisted on the Gwyns to ensure they didn't cross Ives. They jumped Jack and took him to Alan for a hard lesson in local customs. Alan dragged Elizabeth along to watch. Kelly sloped off somewhere. Alan broke Jack's leg with a crowbar then Ives turned up with Kelly. Kelly recognized Jack from somewhere and they took him away to the refrigerated warehouse Alan owned. Meanwhile Alan gave his wife the treatment while Ellis held her.

Alan was moody and concerned for the next few days until Jack Lane was discovered on the mountains. Elizabeth thought there had been some kind of cover-up involving Daniels and Ives, with Ives giving the orders.

Then I came along. She was scared to be seen with me. She told her husband what had happened and Daniels arranged to have me drugged and taken in. From the conversation it seemed that I wasn't to be killed. At least Alan and Daniels did not realize I was for the chop at the time. Ives gave Kelly and Ellis the orders to fix my car with a device he had rigged himself.

The rest of it was piecemeal. Elizabeth had been packed off to Switzerland on the Friday afternoon plane with Kelly and Ellis posing as Ives. From hearing them talking she knew that the plan was to kill me, after decoying me out there and to dispose of her as well. Alan was bored with having a faithless wife. Ives was bored with having me on his tail but didn't want to get involved at this stage because he had pressing business in Wales, at the Whitesands Head Base.

One thing bothered me about that. Before Adamson saw me at the Lion Hotel in Glyntywyn on Friday night, talking to Susan, no-one in Ives' camp would have known that I was alive. Unless

Bo Pepper had told them. And I couldn't see Bo doing that when he had passed up the chance to kill me that morning.

Now who was the snitching bastard that let on that the car bomb had failed to get me?

I thought about it for a while. The provisional list was fairly restricted. It included Ames, Mowlam, Lucinda Bellamy and Sir Simon Verity.

Chapter 18

GUNTHER HAD TOLD me he didn't want any more killing. I promised him there would not be any further fatalities if Ellis made all the right moves.

The Audi drove up to the front of the house. Gunther's lads had taken the utility Volkswagen away. I waited inside the front door for Ellis to ring the bell. He walked in through the door as I opened it and hit him on the base of the neck with the butt of the Magnum. He went down, stunned but not unconscious.

I had learned years ago to keep any personal feelings hidden in confrontations like this one. I needed to approach each one on a purely mechanical level, dispassionately, so I could out-think my suspect and therefore outmanoeuvre him. But the incident in the police station kept coming back to me. I could still feel the pain in my ribs where he had hit me. And I knew he had hurt old Jack.

But Ellis was just a bully boy, good when the odds were on his side. Otherwise he was just another lump of stupid muscle, keen to preserve his own skin. He was no killer. But the mess on the stairs and by the doorway, where the two minders had died, told him I was.

"Your little plan failed. Two dead on your side. Not a mark on me."

He struggled to his feet. I had holstered the Magnum. We faced

139

each other and Ellis's heavy-boned face looked grim and his blue eyes hostile. The heavy mouth was set in a clenched-teeth scowl and he was working out his chances against me.

I did not wait. I kicked him as hard as I could straight in the groin.

"What were you supposed to do when I was dead?"

He would not answer. Two minutes later he was spitting blood and the odd tooth and his left eye was closing up. He outweighed me considerably but I was angry. He had watched while they took Jack and he had held Elizabeth while her husband laid into her. Suddenly he wasn't so tough.

"We're even for that kicking you gave me in the warehouse. Would you like me to give you some more on behalf of Jack Lane and Mrs Gwyn?"

He held up his hands. I searched him and found a lot of money, dollars. Over twenty thousand pounds in all. I felt insulted by Ives. The Bulgarians had once put over twice that on my head until I pointed out to them the error of their ways.

Ellis talked. He did not have a great deal to add. You never tell the hired muscle the finer points. It confuses their simple minds. Kelly had returned to London because he was needed in Wales.

We continued the discussion in one of Gunther's holding cells. There was no more violence because Ellis was terrified and Gunther was a better interrogator than I was. Ellis basically confirmed Elizabeth's story with one important addition: Kelly had recognized Jack Lane from one of Jack's previous tours of duty in Ulster, when Kelly had been lifted by the Security forces and Jack was doing some of the interrogation. I knew Kelly's face was familiar. I had seen it on a wanted sheet. Now what the hell was Ives doing mixed up with an Irish terrorist?

Kelly had killed Jack on Ives' instructions. But the ghastly irony of it was that if Kelly had not recognized him, Jack would probably have still been alive. All Alan Gwyn wanted to do was work Jack over for having it off with his faithless wife.

Ellis was supposed to contact Kelly when Elizabeth and I were dead. So I asked Gunther to do something for me. I gave him the form of words Ellis should use when reporting his failure to kill me.

I spent the afternoon sleeping. God I was tired. The stress was beginning to take its toll. I had sorted out the side-issue of the Gwyns' involvement and now I had to find out the real reason for Jack's death. Ives would not have killed a man he knew to be Security, and British Security at that, without needing to cover his tracks about something, or to secure some future skulduggery that was going on.

I bought Gunther a drink in my hotel room that evening. He sat, still in his dark overcoat, with his grey face and bureaucrat's spectacles, chain-smoking his Gitanes, and sipping his whisky which contained just a little water.

"You won't be coming back here for some time," he announced. It wasn't a question.

"Zurich is too well-fed and humourless for me. Thanks for what you did."

He waved his hand dismissively.

"I owed you a kindness, H. We Swiss like to repay our debts. Call me when you have solved your problem. I would like to think that the men who work on the streets and not their politically-minded controllers won this one."

I returned to London on the early-morning flight. I had written more reports and posted them to Lucinda Bellamy and my solicitor friend. No, I wasn't paperwork mad, just covering myself against the time when it all blew up in my face. And it would. I had this crazy theory that the world was watching me stumbling around after Ives and that maybe I was not alone in wanting to put him out of business. What I couldn't work out was why the C.I.A. in Zurich had intercepted a man who was obviously Ives' watcher. Especially when the N.S.A., in the person of Harman S. Talbot, was dropping obvious hints about how I should stay out of the game. It didn't add up — unless . . .

Something Gunther had said about the Donoghue Corporation and Ives going private set me thinking. So I made a couple of phone calls and at 10.32 am I was in the heart of that other jungle, the City of London. I had arranged a meeting with Carmody who was the fount of all financial knowledge.

He worked in a prestige office building that was architect-designed, had commissioned murals in the foyer, security men from the Corps of Commissaires and was staffed with bi-lingual secretaries who shopped in Harrods.

Carmody's private reception office exuded the hushed and reverential atmosphere of somewhere that handled fortunes. The only sound audible was the discreet shudder of some kind of electronic processor. The only interruptions were those of shirt-sleeved young men with earnest faces and economics degrees who were doing a brisk trade in beige folders marked 'Confidential'.

The secretary was a Home Counties type with a discreet telephone voice and enormous eyes. She gave me black coffee and a smiled reassurance that Carmody knew I was waiting but had taken an urgent call from the Far East. The Hong Kong Exchange had been volatile. It took me ten minutes to realize she was not talking about the telephone system. I watched her for the next twenty minutes, fascinated by those enormous eyes. Then she took me into Carmody's office.

Shirtsleeved himself, surrounded by desk, teleprinter, visual display unit, five telephones and a full ashtray he was talking on two lines simultaneously. I sat down in three inches of padded leather. Carmody smiled at the girl who emptied his ashtray for him and left us alone.

"Hang Seng is up forty," Carmody spoke deliberately into one phone. "Ten million into dollars at one sixty one twenty. Four million into Swiss francs. My price not yours. And to you, Charles."

He picked up an internal phone:

"Marcus. Up the bid on Associated twenty pence cash and insert the usual notice to shareholders in the heavies plus the Mail. No Marcus, twenty is enough. Francis is making a final stab at convincing their chairman but it's not really on. Marcus, sod the Monopolies. They won't accept referral. Talk to you later."

Carmody put the phone down, looked at his watch, and said:

"I can give you five minutes, guru of gunfire."

I knew Carmody because we shot together. Not potting driven pheasants on someone's estate four days a year, but the proper stuff — combat pistol shooting at a North London club. The only reason I carry a gun is that I can really use it. And that takes practice, lots of practice, and more than I get on the section's range. I had given Carmody a lot of pointers that weren't in the instruction manual because he was keen and one day he would be very good. Not as good as me because I would never show him that much. But he appreciated the training. If any intruder tried to burgle the ample Carmody residence outside Croydon, they wouldn't. And in return, Carmody was a source of information in the financial and industrial world that was second to none.

"Desmond Donoghue of the Five D's Corporation. Businesses and personality."

Carmody spoke out of the corner of a straight, narrow mouth. He always wore a cynical half-smile with his business suit. Late forties, fair-haired, he looked like the average well-heeled commuter. And behind the bland face was a brain like a calculator that could compute Deutschmarks into dollars via Japanese yen and back again and still know the commission payable to two decimal points.

"The Bible on that one," he replied. "Diverse interests from cement to chemicals, from real estate to banking and cannon to commodities. Citizen Kane's big brother with shamrocks on."

"So, a lot of clout. Would he use it?"

"Certainly, and he'd make Hitler look like a Liberal. Funds one of the American parties almost single-handed. His hobby is rampaging around the Capitol trying to block U.S. contracts with Britain. He says Ulster is under the heel of the Gestapo and foreign domination. Very proud of the fact that his father was in the old I.R.A. Wasn't, of course. The Americans try to play him down and pretend he is a senile eccentric that no-one listens to. Wrong. He could swing a government."

"How?"

Carmody half-smiled, as if he were dealing with a slow-witted tortoise.

"Really, Halloran. You don't think that people like us allow people like you to have the governments you want, do you? You, Joe Public, might elect them. We bring 'em down, you see. All to do with money and what suits those of us who control or have a lot of it."

"So you think Donoghue can swing the American government? I thought it was only newspapers at Watergate time that did that."

"Who do you think controlled the newspapers?"

"Point taken."

Carmody shook his head slowly. A telephone rang and he picked it up.

"One more favour. Can I borrow your research people to check on Donoghue's interests?"

"Be my guest. My secretary will take you down. Keep your hands to yourself, though. She is a second dan judokai."

Oliver was the resident American business analyst. He wore an Old Wykehamists' tie, close-cropped fair hair and strong after-shave. I asked the questions and he answered in clipped responses, like a machine-gun firing in short bursts.

"Rundown on all business operations carried out by Donoghue's companies?"

"I'll ask the computer. That will give you a quick answer."

It did, on reams of print-out paper. I was looking for two correlating factors, well, correlating as far as my theory went. The first one was still on the classified list at the Pentagon. It was a hand-held surface-to-air missile that made the Soviet SAM 7 look like a boomerang. Manufactured by Donoghue Delta Five Armaments of New Haven, Connecticut, it was known as the Arrowhead. In the same family, but on the anti-tank side of things, was the Sandbagger.

The second correlating factor I was looking for was any business or property owned by the Donoghue empire in the Republic of Eire. There were a dozen, ranging from crane factories to a space research laboratory. Only two of these locations were on the coast: one at Cork, the other at Ballymurtagh.

Geography was never my strong point. I asked Oliver if he happened to know where Ballymurtagh was.

"County Kerry, old man."

I wasn't so keen on the old man part, especially as Oliver only looked twenty.

"Where exactly?"

"Situated on the north-east coast of a two-mile promontory jutting north from the peninsula that points westward above Dingle Bay. The research facility is situated on the shore line of a U-shaped inlet something similar to a Norwegian fiord. You know where Norway is? Sorry, silly joke. The countryside around there is beautiful. Ballymurtagh, I mean. Walk for miles and not see anyone."

"Know it well?"

"Family owned most of it at the turn of the century. Had to leave because of the troubles. Burnt the house."

"What do they research?"

"Civil satellite projects. The Space division is developing instrumentation modules for monitoring weather, relaying television and telephone systems. Third-generation stuff. It could also have applications such as the Star Wars option — capability of neutralizing incoming missiles."

"Is that feasible?"

"Indeed. Do you know that they now have satellites that can listen in to my phone calls to the New York Office?"

"Really. That is frightening."

"Makes you think."

"So Ballymurtagh would be a restricted sort of place?"

"Certainly. And the location is ideal. Nearest village is four miles away, place called Nagleton. They are as poor as your compulsory ethnic minority out there. Dublin are delighted to see Donoghue in Ireland. He already has plans for three more factories there. And he owns agricultural land. Numbers twenty-eight to thirty on your printout."

"Thanks, Oliver."

"What line are you in?" he asked casually.

"Investigative journalism," I lied.

As I left the City by taxi I couldn't help thinking that everyone knew what I was doing except me. The C.I.A. had been there to intercept Ives' man at Zurich. It was almost as if someone was telegraphing my moves to the Americans. And the Americans fell into two distinct categories. Ives and the N.S.A. generally hostile to the Halloran existence. C.I.A. neutral, or on at least two occasions in favour of Halloran carrying on.

Something Goldstein had said to me at the party that night was playing on my mind. Something about Lucinda Bellamy's temperament. I decided to have a word with Goldstein.

He had the flu and was tucked up in bed chez Aunt Rachel in Golders Green. The Portuguese maid was handing him hot toddies while Aunt Rachel fussed around laying out his papers on the bedside table. Goldstein was loving every minute of it.

"Why didn't you bring grapes?" he demanded, his spectacles misted up with the condensation from the hot whisky.

"I considered flowers but they didn't have any dandelions."

"Well, why are you bothering me? Can't you see I'm ill?"

Aunt Rachel raised her dark and mysterious eyes to the ceiling and shooed the maid out. I liked Aunt Rachel. She had a fine sense of the ridiculous.

"You can only have five minutes," she announced grandly, playing to the Goldstein ego. Then quietly to me as she passed: "I should be so fortunate."

"Don't smoke in here," Goldstein objected. "This is a sick room."

I avoided the obvious comment. Getting cheap laughs out of Goldstein got boring after a while. He was more than usually grey. Then I looked grey compared to the garish hue of his pyjamas.

"Polish your spectacles and pay attention. Ever seen this man before?"

He took Ives' photograph and examined it carefully.

"Previous boyfriend of Lucinda Bellamy's by any chance?"

Goldstein shook his head. Another Halloran theory gone west.

"Tell me everything you know, in detail, about the lovely Lucinda."

"Why should I?" Goldstein demanded. He was enjoying himself. He had something I wanted. Raising the whisky glass he grinned smugly.

"Because you already have the flu and a constricted windpipe will aggravate your weakened condition."

"If you put it like that, ask ahead. . . . "

In *Julius Caesar*, by W. Shakespeare, there is a line that goes something like: 'There is a tide in the affairs of men which taken at the flood leads on to victory.' I think it was Cassius who said it and look what happened to him. He ended up on the point of his own sword. If I wasn't very careful that would happen to me.

I needed to know what was happening in the Hall of Mirrors and what the Star Chamber's attitude now was to me. Which meant I had to contact Ames. I took the chance and rang his office.

"This is your favourite old age pensioner here. I need an urgent meet. Are you free?"

"Usual place. Half an hour."

Ames was as good as his word. We met in the Imperial War Museum. Ames liked the Imperial War Museum. Perhaps they had first option on his mortal remains to be stuffed and put in a glass case marked 'Anonymous Intelligence Man. Ulster 1973'. He was ambling past the display of infantry weapons when I tapped him on the shoulder.

"So you're still in one piece. The N.S.A. have been making threats against your person. I have it on good authority that Mowlam has denied you, unofficially of course."

Which meant that if I fell under a bus, Mowlam wouldn't invoke sanctions against his allies. If I was found shot dead within a mile radius of Grosvenor Square he would be forced to take action. That attitude was as of that morning, 8.00 am Monday 3 February.

"Sounds about right. You've got a photographic memory, pardon the pun. Take a look at this mugshot going under the name of Liam Kelly. Ex-I.R.A. late Sixties, early Seventies. Your time out there. Jack Lane's time out there. He'd have been just a lad then. But he recognized Jack. That's why they killed him. Not because he had given away his interest in Natasha Madsen. That came after the bastards scopolamined him."

Ames took the photograph and nodded.

"I know the little excrescence. Name of Seamus Rafferty. Skipped to the States after killing three young Guardsmen in a tart

147

trap. Killed the tarts as well. He's had a face job, but I'd know those eyes anywhere. Where does he fit in?"

"I believe he has Jack Lane's Browning. I'm not saying any more because it's better you don't know. Mowlam is using me on this one and I'll need all my talents to stay in one piece after I've cracked it. Find out from Northern Ireland what the word is on sophisticated toys getting to the I.R.A. or any splinter groups. I'll be in touch usual time and rendezvous. And don't fuss. I'm still the best there is in this goddamn business and don't you ever forget it."

Ames had a faraway look in his eyes. He had gone back ten years to the backstreets of Belfast and the grimiest war he had ever fought. One day we would have our own My Lai over there. Then he looked seriously at me and said:

"Just you watch yourself. If you need any help, shout. And when you take Jack's Browning back from Rafferty or whatever the bastard calls himself these days, empty a full magazine into him at point blank range and give him my love."

Chapter 19

EAST ANGLIA IS flat. And to someone whose childhood was spent in the mountains it was a strange world. A clump of trees became intensely interesting because it broke the skyline's continuous monotony.

The airfield was two miles from the nearest village. Unused since the Americans flew B 24 Liberators from its now crumbling runways in another age, it was drab, grey and cold. The east wind blowing that day must have come straight across from the Urals, clean across Europe and the North Sea to send a chill into my bones. Even the entrance gates had rusted away and the grass beside the runways was dry and withered. In the middle distance, low concrete buildings huddled together and the old control tower stood upright and tall in contrast, defying the wind, a scarred monument to a bygone era. The hangars had long gone, taken down for scrap or purloined by chicken farmers.

I hid the car between two of the longer buildings, crew quarters I guessed. I climbed the derelict tower, its rusted handrails none too steady, and was satisfied with my vantage point. High ground. Always make the high ground.

I had over an hour to wait. So I lit a cigarillo and inhaled the dark taste of the tobacco. It reminded me of Mowlam's soul. But I would have the chance to rub his nose in it later on. If I was still around.

Kelly was coming to see me. He had to because they had failed to get me in Zurich. The longer I survived, the more chance I had of working out Ives' misdeeds. Ives could not afford that. Maybe Ives himself would come, to ensure the job was done properly, but I doubted that. He would not risk coming out into the open. He was a really professional operator who would use Kelly for the donkey work. I needed Kelly in one piece just long enough to ask him one or two pertinent questions. Then I would kill him for squealing on Jack Lane and taking part in his killing.

Gunther had taken care of the invitation and it was couched in my own form of words to be delivered by Ellis, with Gunther standing over him. The story was that I had escaped injury in Zurich but was flying back by private charter to the East Anglian airfield with Elizabeth Gwyn in tow. And we were ready to talk about what we knew to the appropriate people.

I reckoned Ives was doing private work for Donoghue using his position in the N.S.A. I was counting on the fact that his superiors would take a dim view of this. So Ives' tactic would be to have Kelly and some hired help turn up at the airfield to put me out of business. I had only one problem — staying alive through the encounter.

For fifteen years I had known that the day my number was up, it would be in some out-of-the-way place like this. A desolate patch of concrete would be stained with the Halloran lifeblood ebbing away as I lay paralysed and all smashed-up inside. Just like in that dream I'd been having. Yet at least if they got me today I would have the satisfaction of really knowing why. You never beat the system. The nearest you get is knowing how it works. This time I had glimpsed into the Hall of Mirrors. I knew why the Star Chamber had used Jack Lane and then me in furthering its crazy conspiratorial schemes. They threatened my very survival, but they were just chess games to Mowlam and the men who controlled Ives.

I opened the back door of the Volvo. A fully-equipped vehicle I had asked for, and Ames had done his stuff. I took out the boxed multi-channel radio transmitter/receiver that would enable me to eavesdrop on all two-way radio conversations in the immediate area. I knew the channels the C.I.A. and N.S.A. used as well they knew ours. And if I was wrong about Kelly coming with the hired help and it was a genuine N.S.A. attack on the Halloran, I would know about it. Because that device enabled me to pick up any extraneous chatter from any vehicles they would use up to twenty miles out. Then I would be out again to the Volvo calling up police assistance on the emergency frequency of a second, similar device fitted as standard in the estate car. Of course I would have some explaining to do. Everyone would be covered in embarrassment. It would provoke a major inter-allied incident. But I would still be in one piece. The odds were against that eventuality occurring. I reckoned that if Ives kept pressing for my head on an official platter, someone would start asking him awkward questions.

I set the portable R.T. up in the control tower and returned to the Volvo for the two suitcases. Never a good idea to be heroic and stand the odds off single-handed, but at least I had come prepared. So watch out, Kelly. It wasn't Jack Lane you were looking for this time. It was Halloran. And on a scale of ten as a mean street-fighter, Halloran rated eleven and one half.

I loaded the Ithaca twelve-gauge riot gun, the one with the folding stock and slide action. It took five cartridges, each a three-inch cased load stuffed with an ounce and three quarters of oo buckshot that would take an opponent's head off at twenty yards. Next came the spare forty-one Magnum. This one had the eight-and-three-quarter-inch barrel on it. Ammunition was the maximum ballistic load the weapon would take. For the slightly longer-range work. Together with six portions of my favourite dessert — pineapple surprise — and a flak jacket that would stop most short cartridges, I waited for something to happen.

By 3.26 pm I was getting bored and nervous. The waiting was like hanging around a branch railway station, for a train you knew had to come, to take you somewhere important, and no-one had told you what time it came in. I lit my fourth cigarillo and regretted missing lunch. I said 'Hello' to the flight controllers and watched the Liberators taxi out for take-off, bristling with fifty-calibre Browning machine-guns, their steel bellies replete with high explosive. I heard the roar of the engines and the crackling of radio voices and watched as the bombers lumbered slowly into the air at the end of the thousand-yard runway. I was not alone, but the last in a long line of men who had waited in that exposed control tower for something to happen.

I scanned the far-off road with my binoculars. The traffic was infrequent. A sausage van sped along urgently to be followed ten minutes later by a tractor whose driver, high in the safety cab, watched the land and did not seem at all concerned with the road. I walked up and down the steps for a while, unable to concentrate on anything except how many friends Kelly would bring with him. They knew I had done two already, so my guess was they would double for safety. Say Kelly and three others.

They would probably come in close to occupy the control tower. There wasn't much cover around the perimeter fence except a line of trees about two hundred yards from the tower. A good place for a sniper to hide. He could cover the runways and the entrance to the airfield from there as well as back up anyone occupying the tower. The more I looked at this line of trees the greater the realization became. I would be in trouble from a rifleman out there. And I had not brought a rifle.

The Smith & Wesson .41 Magnum with the long barrel was the next best thing. And I had brought its detachable shoulder stock and scope. Harry had made the shoulder stock for me and it had not been an easy task. The four-power telescopic sight needed mountings specially drilled for it in the Magnum's frame, so Harry had come up with the ingenious idea of attaching screw-tightened clamps to the scope which would fit over the Magnum's top strap. In less than three minutes I had assembled the attachments and fitted them on the Magnum. I was ready to ensure the scope was sighted in correctly when the chance had gone.

A blue transit van meandered along the roadway and turned in through the entrance. Through the binoculars I could see one unidentified man driving and Kelly sitting alongside him in the front. They looked like a couple of blue-overalled repair men except that Kelly was looking around anxiously with far greater concern than he would have shown if he were just looking out for a delivery address.

The transit stopped. One man got out of the back and I noticed the case slung over his shoulder. It was a gun case and he had no binoculars with him. That meant the long gun was probably a scoped rifle. Not good. He had probably zeroed his rifle in already. I watched him scamper off into the long grass and disappear from view.

Kelly had shown his hand now. I crouched by the open door of the control tower, Ithaca in hand. I worked the slide to shove one up the spout. The range was closing. Eighty, sixty, forty, twenty yards. By the time they were in a position to see my car between the buildings it was too late.

I let go three fast shots. One through the windscreen and one through the driver's door. The third went in the general area of the offside front tyre. Have some of that, you bastards! The blast rolled into a crescendo of deafening sound as the echo bounced around the walls of my hiding place. The windscreen shattered, the tyre exploded and the transit slewed front end on to face me.

Hellfire! Anyone in the back could use the van for cover while getting out. The horn kept sounding like a heavy object was jammed against it. I had probably got the driver. I let go two more shots from the Ithaca then the ejection port locked open.

I pulled the short Magnum out and fired fast through the roof of the transit to where I thought any more backseat passengers might be. But it was their turn to dish it out now. The sniper on the perimeter opened up with a burst of accurate automatic fire that sent concrete chips splintering around my head and stinging into my face. I ducked back inside the doorway. That sniper was good! An Irish voice yelled "Cover." I had already stuffed more cartridges into the Ithaca. Now a movement near the corner of the barrack building attracted my attention. The slightest movement in such circumstances can mean you're about to be outflanked. I sent two more shots after it and missed.

Then their combined firepower started giving me the treatment and the nasty stuff was ricocheting around like balls in a pinball machine. The sniper was having fun, so was the man with a sub-machine-gun. And for good measure, someone threw in four fast shots from a handgun.

But that control tower had been built to last. They could chip away at the walls all day with small-arms fire and still not penetrate the walls. There was only one way in and that was the way I had come. Up the steps and in through the open doorway. And I could cover that and take them out one at a time as they came up. Of course it was my only way out, but I knew that before I started.

There was a lull in the lethal cacophony as they changed magazines and no doubt had a mothers' meeting about what to do next. I reckoned there were only three left alive: the sniper and two men in close. Then Kelly shouted:

"We can wait all bloody night."

"You can't put any civilians in the way, this time, you retarded bogtrotter," I shouted back. "You're just like the rest of those skulking alley rats hiding behind their women's skirts. You haven't got the balls for a real fight."

I was trying to anger him and I had succeeded. He went bananas and loosed off an entire magazine. That's my boy, Kelly. Gunfighting is an art for the thinking man. Go on, keep losing your cool.

I was prone now, parallel to the doorway and tight to the outer wall. I had a very narrow slit of vision from an oblique angle to the opening. I risked moving forward just enough to get a look at the perimeter man through the binoculars. He was belly down by the trees, adjusting his scope. I had been careless in not bringing a sniper's rifle. The shotgun was useless after fifty yards and my short forty-one Magnum would not make the distance accurately enough. But a long-barrelled pistol is better than you think. So I reached for the scoped Magnum.

Someone rushing for the control tower wall distracted me. I wasn't having any of that nonsense. They could have grenades. So I took one of my pineapple surprises and pulled the pin, depressed the cocking lever and counted to three. Then I lobbed them a gift through the open doorway. The sniper potted at me but the sound of his burst was lost in a shattering explosion. Six-second fuse on my pineapple surprises. Not long enough to realize what was going to hit them.

In theory you can never get out of range of a grenade on flat ground. The explosive charge shatters its metal casing and scatters myriads of metal shards around. It is a weapon for killing in enclosed spaces like a foxhole or a room where the walls contain the damage within. They also have the effect of protecting the thrower. The wall of the control tower protected me. But the simpleton who had used the same wall for cover, thirty feet below me, had been badly hit. I could hear him screaming.

Kelly was angry again. More sub-machine-gun fire. But my real problem was that sniper on the perimeter. He could pin me down while Kelly rushed the stairway to the tower. If Kelly had enough guts, that was. Alternatively, he would wait to pick me off if I was careless enough to stick my head out.

I sneaked a look through the binoculars again. By now the sniper had realized I was shotgun armed. He was now standing upright using a tree branch for a rest, waiting for the next opportunity to get a really accurate shot at me.

There had been no chance of hitting him as he lay prone, but now he was a target. I reached for the long-barrelled Magnum. It was capable of hitting targets up to three hundred yards away. Okay, lucky shots, some of them, but possible.

My hands were damp as I squeezed the detachable stock into my shoulder. My breathing was quick and excitable and my hands shook. I told myself to calm down, take it slow and easy, take the correct position and fire when my breath was two-thirds out. Just like they taught you in the Army.

The cross-hairs of the scope centred on his middle. This was a risky shot. If I missed and he realized I had the capability to reach him I would get no second chance. I squeezed the trigger, very gently.

The Magnum bucked. For a split second I thought I had blown it. The report rolled around the walls. Then I saw him, in full-frontal glory, arms spread wide, his feet a good foot off the ground. The heavy bullet had caught him amidships, two hundred yards from where I had fired, the impact smashed him backwards six feet and dumped him against a tree stump. There was no need for a second shot. Through the scope I could see his head hanging lifelessly.

Now my hands were shaking, with relief and elation. Got you, you bastard. Two hundred bloody yards away and I got you! Now for Kelly.

The silence from outside was unhealthy. He would be behind the barracks somewhere. Or was he? Minutes passed slowly, or so it seemed. In reality it was only a few seconds. I loaded up all the weaponry again. Then a voice called.

"Halloran, it's just the two of us left."

"Not for long Kelly. It's three nil to me and you're in borrowed time."

"Man, this is crazy. We can talk a deal."

"Yes, like you chucking your hardware out and walking into the open."

His voice gave his position away. Somewhere around the right-hand corner of the barracks and probably inside. I moved position for a shot at him. I knew he would be doing the same.

"If I give you the book on Ives, will you let me go?"

"After you pulled this stunt?"

"Not my idea. Ives' man in the trees called the shots. You need to know what goes on, Halloran. If not, sure as hell they'll get you."

He did have a point. It sounded like a reasonable deal.

"Show yourself, Kelly. Back off into the open, by the van but not too close."

"Will do," he replied.

A door closed and five seconds later he was there. Faintly

ridiculous in large overalls, he held out his hands and backed towards the van.

I stood up but the Ithaca was still in my hands. I didn't believe he was serious. He had some trick up his sleeve. But how the hell was he going to work it? He would never outdraw and beat me to the shot at thirty yards. He could not get closer to the transit without crossing my line of fire. But there was another means of escape — my Volvo. Okay, so Kelly would have to break in and hot-wire the car to start it. But it was well out of my sight. And by the time I had got myself into a position to shoot at it, Kelly should be two hundred yards away and accelerating. And for an Ulster boy, hot-wiring a car was second nature to Kelly. So why hadn't Kelly taken his chance? I would have done. Then again maybe I would have hung around, if I had a killing plan.

The split second that I walked through that open doorway I knew. The shrapnelled man by the wall. Bloodied and dying though he was, he was strong enough to raise the handgun. I fired three times. The sprayed lead that didn't kill him chipped puffs of dust out of the concrete like hailstones hitting water.

Pivotting on the balls of my feet I turned to face Kelly. He was standing up straight, a pistol half-out of his overalls. Forty feet was the range, close enough for me to see the terrible realization on his face that his dirty trick had failed, as he was about to fail in the business of living. The impact of the two shots smashed him to the concrete. I ran down the steps of the control tower towards him.

No-one else was left standing except me.

Kelly was still alive. Both patterns had peppered him from the stomach down. His outstretched hand opened and closed frantically. I stood over him, Ithaca already reloaded. There was no need. He could barely speak. Further resistance was impossible.

"Ives said you'd take some killing," he gasped. "Jesus, Halloran, I'm hurt. Mary, Mother of Mercy. There's a thousand red-hot needles burning inside of me."

His leg twitched in spasmodic agony. The eyes hated me but the lips laughed. And on the ground, out of his reach, was a GP35 automatic, the one he had failed to kill me with. It was familiar to me. I had found Jack Lane's Browning.

For the first time since the firefight started I lost control. It was seeing Jack's gun that did it. My finger tightened on the trigger of the Ithaca and I wanted to fire and keep firing until Kelly was nothing but disintegrated bits of flesh. Then I would wipe out every trace of him.

"You killed Jack Lane."

"I . . . recognized him . . . see. And he knew me . . . memory like a bloody . . . e . . . elephant. Went back all . . . the way to the . . . good days."

I took sharp hold of myself. Cool it, Halloran. You've killed him. And he's dying with the agony of knowing that Jack's reflex action got him. Then:

"Holy Mary . . . I need a priest. . . . "

Even filth like Kelly believed in something. His curving fingers were clutching at the overall pocket. I knelt over him and took out the rosary. He half-smiled and clutched at it. I took it away from him.

"First things first. What's Ives' game?"

His conscience was wrestling with concern for his immortal soul. Finally he mumbled:

"SAMS . . . bloody SAMS. From the States . . . to Whitesands . . . then to the boys . . . the lovely boys."

"From Whitesands to where exactly?"

"Ballymurtagh."

"Donoghue's place. So it's his operation?"

He nodded, clutching again for the rosary. I had him and he knew it. He would have sold his mother for that rosary.

"Who set it up? Donoghue? Does he have backing?"

"Himself. And no-one can touch him. Fooled you Brits. . . . Ives is the key man . . . transport, you see . . . secret."

Kelly had precious little time left. The patterns of shot had busted him up inside. I dangled the rosary and with a supreme effort he raised both hands to take it. But I was no longer full of blind, unthinking hatred. I could think very clearly now. I snatched the rosary out of his reach and stood up.

"So you worked on Jack Lane and killed him?"

His eyes widened in unspeakable terror. He tried to articulate the word 'Yes' but his voice had gone. He tried to plead with me but I could not hear him.

I smiled and said:

"That's one sin you won't buy absolution for. Have a super time in eternal damnation."

I picked up the Browning and walked away.

Chapter 20

THE ENTIRE ACTION had occupied the space of eleven minutes, although it seemed like a lifetime to me. I packed up the cases and put them in the Volvo. Then I gathered up all my empty cartridges. No need to leave unnecessary clues around for any copper attracted by the sound of gunfire to find. Although nosey locals seemed to be thin on the ground. Lucky for me.

I started the Volvo and was listening in to a police channel when I heard a familiar voice. It was excited and was ordering back-up units from the local firearms squad to converge on the airfield. Ames. Now how had he got in on the act? I decided to cut in on the conversation.

"This is Omega Blue One," I called. "Already in position. The area is secure. One car only required. Omega Leader."

"Omega Blue One," Ames voice replied. "Repeat the message."

"Going deaf in your old age. Omega Blue One already in position. Area is secure. Only Omega Leader required."

I halted by the entrance gates. Ten minutes later, a Jaguar XJS came screaming along the road and pulled up alongside the Volvo in a flurry of dust. Ames leaped out.

"Hello, Ames. You missed the party. Who invited you?"

"Bo Pepper called me. Said you could be in trouble. He had been instructed to follow Kelly but not to intercept or participate. Told me to get a move on if I wanted my number-one man to stay in one

158

piece. I think the C.I.A. have a soft spot for you."

"The hell they have. He was just following orders from some Deputy Director in Langley. I expect he told you not to advertise your source of information?"

"He did. What happened?"

"I've just found Jack Lane's gun. By the way, did you find out about the Irish arms situation?"

"Yes. There is a security blanket on the information but the I.R.A. recently received some American SAMs. The latest gear. Arrowheads and Sandbaggers, according to my impeccable sources. Two helicopters have been downed already. It's serious, very serious. The security forces have been putting pressure on the Northern Ireland Office for months so that our noble political masters will read the Riot Act to the White House, no less."

"Thanks. Has any progress been made?"

"No idea. Mowlam would know all about that. I recall fixing security for a preliminary type visit a couple of months back. Permanent Secretary level. No feedback to me. But there wouldn't be, would there?"

"Get hold of creepy Mowlam and tell him Halloran now knows what the Star Chamber is up to. I'll meet him tonight at a location to be advised later, through you. Tell him alone or the newspapers and anyone else I can think of will have the story and his plan will have backfired. Then he'll have to get another sap to go after Ives."

With that cheery message I engaged the clutch, but said as an afterthought:

"Do me a favour and tidy up the mess over there. Four dead. One is Kelly, or Rafferty, who won't be killing any more of the lads, or any more tarts for that matter. I'll call you at the pub at eight."

I was in a pub at one minute past opening time. I needed the first large Scotch. It didn't hit the sides going down. I could smell cordite but I was alone. My clothes reeked of it. But the smell of death always followed you around long after the gunfire had died down. I ordered another Scotch.

"Hard day?" the landlord inquired.

"You could say that," I replied, put the Scotch down in one and walked out into the darkness.

At eight pm exactly I called Ames and gave him directions for Mowlam, then I added the warning.

"Remind him I can shoot his ears off at forty yards if I even think he's brought company."

Ames replied:

"You can't say things like that to Mowlam. It's blasphemy."

"I don't belong to the Church any more."

Ames was chuckling to himself as he put the phone down.

Harry was lurking in one of those sweaty clubs the Maltese run in Soho. The girl wanted to take twenty quid off me at the door. I was ready to be persuasive when Angelo sloped past, astrakhan-coated, Gauloise dangling from rubber lips, trying hard to pretend he hadn't seen me.

"Angelo," I called. "Don't be so bloody unsociable."

Angelo's minder shuffled into the ready position, ham hands dangling from anthropoid arms. Before he had taken one step forward he had seen the Magnum holstered under my jacket.

"Not today, Josephine," I warned.

Angelo turned, half-smiling, his greasy complexion beaded with globules of perspiration. He was obviously on a collection round.

"Mr Halloran, I didn't see you there." Then to the girl:

"Okay sweetheart, he's with me."

I winked at the girl who did not smile back. Angelo descended the stairs and I followed. The minder stayed a respectful distance from me.

At the dimly-lit bar, Angelo ordered me a drink. The proper article and not the flat bitter stuff they peddled to the punters as Scotch. He smiled insecurely at me and I waved him away. He disappeared into a back room. Angelo had five such places as this. Together with the sex shops, the dirty bookstore, the massage parlours and his overrider on the girls' takings, he netted thirty thousand a week, even when he was inside doing the occasional obligatory twelve months under the obscene publications laws.

Harry was next to the stage where a black stripper was doing amazing things with her white companion and a rhino whip. The humidity, the sweat and the carbon atmosphere was oppressive. I gave an under-age hostess a fiver to go and fetch Harry for me.

His gaze was still fixed on the floorshow. His swivelling eyes glanced at me and then returned to the mass of writhing limbs.

"Your keys, Harry. And don't go near the warehouse tonight."

He handed them over without a word of protest. His mind, if you could call it that, was elsewhere. Topside, the comparative fresh air of the streets was another world.

Harry's warehouse was well situated for observing the comings and goings of visitors while offering ample time for escape. Harry was no fool. He knew the Law would have to drive the hundred-yard cul-de-sac to get at him. By which time he would have 'had it on his toes' across the rooftops via the skylight, and been a street away. Which was my reason for picking that location to meet Mowlam.

I went up to the roof, via the skylight with its well-oiled hinges. The late-night sky was clear and the night-time sounds carried down to the river. I settled behind the low parapet and hunched into my coat. Almost three-quarters of an hour to wait. I noticed the stars looking down on me. I looked back but they didn't notice me at all. I was tired, tense and frightened. Looking at the vast expanse of bright-dotted universe did not exactly imbue me with confidence. It made me feel insignificant, dispensable. And enough people thought I was dispensable already.

Ives' people had tried twice for me and failed. A third attempt on me would be made. That one would be successful because the big boys would all be trying very hard. I would have no friends and even my own side would be very happy to deny me in case I knew too much. As soon as I delivered Ives, the Americans would take me out. Both C.I.A. and N.S.A. would join forces and Mowlam would be delighted to see me go. Because for everyone concerned it would be politically expedient.

On the surface of it, the whole business was bizarre, crazy, incredible even. But in fifteen years in my business I had learned that survival on the streets was only one essential. You had to work out where Ames and the others from the Hall of Mirrors stood. But vitally, if you ever got involved with the Veritys and the Mowlams, the conspirators of the Star Chamber, you had to know what they were playing at in order to survive. And they played in the rarefied stratosphere of global and international politics where the poor bloody infantry like Halloran were never allowed or even considered as being capable of any kind of independent thought. If the time ever came when they realized the rules and objectives of any particular game, they were removed from the field of play, permanently.

They would remove me in this case as a precaution against my ever working out what it was really all for. But I was two steps ahead of the Intelligence establishments this time. And I would trade that fact with Mowlam for my continued safe existence.

The Americans had been playing games. They had wanted someone else to do their dirty work for them and provide the patsy to keep everyone happy. Mowlam and Verity had used first Jack Lane and now me in the role of expendable sucker. I was not surprised. Fifteen years in my business had sent me out into the world with no illusions. The Star Chamber had a job to do. It was not really justified on any moral grounds. Nothing ever really is. It was a question of expediency and staying two steps ahead of everyone else. I had finally learned to play the game. The irony of it was, I was too late, if the Star Chambers on both sides of the Atlantic had their way.

Natasha Madsen had been sent in to Whitesands and the Glyntywyn area by a Deputy Director of Langley, Virginia, C.I.A. headquarters. You read in the Press that the Intelligence organizations are run by a bunch of half-wits who don't know what they are doing. Wrong. It is part of the Hall of Mirrors syndrome. You see what they want you to see. Natasha Madsen was the wrong choice because of her cover as a disarmament worker and because of her inexperience. Therefore they had not expected her to succeed. Therefore they wanted her to fail and had probably tipped Ives off themselves. They needed her dead body to provoke her stepfather, Sir Simon Verity, into action. They had even forbidden Bo Pepper and the London Station C.I.A. boys to investigate. Bo had tried to sell me the idea it was some kind of inter-agency war. It wasn't. Both C.I.A. and probably the top brass in the N.S.A. wanted the British to look into the girl's death. What better way than to murder Natasha Madsen? Because sending a young girl to operate in Ives' territory was murder.

They probably reckoned on Verity sending someone in unofficially. As it was Verity had obviously consulted Mowlam. They had probably asked themselves the same questions I had, then played along. Jack Lane was the obvious choice. He was expendable. If Jack failed to make it back with the answer, they would send someone else, upping the stakes all the time, until they could legitimately hold up their hands in horror and launch a full-scale official probe, sending in the cavalry as I had wanted Verity to do. I was ideal material because I was retired, had recently been on a stress evaluation course and was there as a sacrificial lamb to the Americans if I succeeded in getting Ives. I was meant to get Ives, and I would.

Now it seemed crazy that the Americans really wanted Ives out of the way but wanted the blame placed elsewhere. Until I realized that he was running SAMs to the Micks under cover of official transport to a clandestine N.S.A. base in Eire. Ives was doing this for that ageing homicidal leprechaun Desmond Donoghue. I guessed the N.S.A. had discovered this. But they themselves were not exactly in a position to lay down the law. Because Donoghue had provided them with a facility inside his research establishment at Ballymurtagh. He could withdraw that facility and also threaten his political clients with withdrawal of support. It was election year Stateside and the Irish vote was a large one. And if Donoghue made an issue out of it, well . . .

Now what would happen when Ives was killed? Donoghue would be wild because his key man in the secret transportation system would have been taken out. He would find it very hard to recruit any more. The Counter-Intelligence boys would scotch that one. The N.S.A. could throw up their hands in horror and explain that a vengeful lunatic ex-British agent named Halloran had killed Ives for removing Jack Lane. Verity and Mowlam would provide the details of my insanity. The N.S.A. would take me out. They had already established the principle when Harman S. Talbot announced it to Sean. Mowlam had given his tacit approval so all the players would be dead and only the conspirators would know the real truth.

The C.I.A. had, of course, twice saved me. Because they and the N.S.A. top brass wanted me to succeed in getting Ives. They had delayed my follower at Zurich airport. They had been keeping tabs on Ives and Kelly. And good old Bo Pepper had been doing Good Samaritan impersonations to Ames.

As I sat there, another thought struck me. All this had probably come about because we were putting political pressure on the Americans to do something about the gun-running to the Irish. Maybe it was the Americans' way of making life hard for us by leaving us with the blame.

A dirty, squalid affair all round. But weren't they all? Fifteen years in the business had taught me at least that much. I had nailed Kelly for killing Jack Lane and I would have Ives. But it was Mowlam and Verity who had sent him in, knowing he was cannon fodder. And the Americans were just as guilty because they knew Ives had something to hide. In my own way maybe I too was guilty for not having kept in touch with him sufficiently to dissuade him from going in to reclaim his lost reputation. But if you are the best it is always hard to accept the time when you are not. Which was why I was going out at the best time, before I started sliding downhill like Jack had done. If Mowlam would let me.

At two minutes to midnight, a dark Vanden Plas pulled into the street and waited, as directed, beneath the street light. Headlights flashed four times and were turned off. I flashed my torch twice in response and moved position. The seconds seemed to go by very slowly. I could hear my anxious breathing. The butt of the Magnum felt comfortable in my hand.

The car's rear door opened and the thin figure of Mowlam emerged, hatless and in dark overcoat. I could make out his sunken-eyed expression with the aid of the night glasses. In one hand he held a torch and in the other glowed a lighted cigar. He walked forward steadily, looking neither right nor left but straight at the door of the warehouse which I had left half-open.

I swung myself through the skylight on to the wooden landing. The warehouse door closed. A torch flashed and started waving crazy patterns in the darkness as he looked around. I flicked the light switches on. He blinked, momentarily dazzled by the sudden illumination. I remained at the top of the spiral staircase.

"Is all this really necessary?" he asked and glanced disdainfully at the assorted boxes and crates, the dust and the litter.

"Come on up," I invited. "The perspective is very different from where I am standing."

I forced myself to sound confident, in control. Mowlam worried me more than all the Kellys of this world and more than Ives. Because Mowlam was clever enough to run rings around me. He knew more. And knowledge was power in this game.

He climbed the staircase slowly. His coat was open. Underneath the silk scarf and the evening suit told me I had disturbed a formal occasion. What the hell? He had disturbed my life. He looked straight through me and announced:

"You should be reporting to Verity."

He looked more like a living corpse than ever in the bright lights. His eyes still screwed up occasionally. The lines on his forehead were as prominent as if they had been stage make-up.

"I'm reporting to you. So pay attention."

Mowlam wasn't too pleased with my attitude.

"While I may be pleasantly surprised at your continued survival I do not like your threats about running to the Press. Threats like that are criminal."

"So are you Mowlam. Now make yourself comfortable while I tell you the story."

He listened, as I went through my reasoning, stage by stage. He puffed unconcernedly on his cigar when I came to the best bit about how he had used everyone. When I accused him of cooking this up in conjunction with the Americans he smiled.

"I guessed what they were up to when Verity came to see me about his stepdaughter's death. Our transatlantic cousins had counted on Simon doing something unofficially, thereby fooling us into an unofficial operation against one of their men. This would have given them the opportunity of thinking they had something on us they could use for trade at a future date. Sometimes you know I think we'd all be better off reaching an accommodation with the

K.G.B. At least I understand their particularly underhand way of doing things. But I can still bring it off, can't I? The Americans don't know that you are working with official sanction. I have tried to keep it from them."

"Even to the extent of letting them kill me when I have delivered Ives to you?"

"Regrettably, yes. Nothing personal in it, Halloran. I'm impressed with you. But you're leaving us and well . . . " he waved his hand in a dismissive gesture.

"There's something you ought to know, Sir Maurice. The Americans have someone inside our camp who knows exactly what's going on."

"You can't be serious?" he said, surprised and worried now.

"I don't know when you last spoke with old Rigby at Internal Security but he had the means to discover the fact."

Mowlam screwed his eyes up again, this time in disapproval at the thought of having anything to do with an outfit like Internal Security.

"Go on," he invited.

"We come to that later. All I want to do is get out of this business in one piece. Life is not perfect but I'd like to give it a try for the next few years. You want Ives and I can deliver him. My terms. I want one man for back-up. I also want you to instruct the Americans that Halloran is bloody sacred and that if I so much as catch cold you'll have someone's balls. In return you get Ives and the American insider and I don't go to the Press or anyone else like the Americans with the tale that you really know what was going on."

I had given it my best shot. Mowlam did not smile but said only:

"Our political masters have been pressuring the White House for some time to halt the arms flow to Ireland. All this is the result of that pressure. The Americans have gone about it in circuitous fashion. We don't want them embarrassed by failure. Remember Halloran, if this stunt of yours does not come off we are back to square one with the problem. And if the P.M. ever found out that I had anything to do with messing up the chance to win then I would be running a quango in the Hebrides. And if that happens, Halloran, you won't have the Americans to worry about. I'll come after you myself, in person, and I'll bring half the S.A.S. with me."

Then Mowlam smiled. We had reached an understanding.

Chapter 21

AFTER A FURTHER half-hour's conversation with Mowlam I arrived at Lucinda's flat. I didn't want to go back to my place in case anyone was watching. There was no point in taking unnecessary risks at this stage. Besides, Lucinda had invited me and I never turned down invitations that good.

The following morning I woke early, in a cold sweat. The bad dream again, the one where I got shot. But this time it was so real I woke up shouting.

Lucinda must have been awake already. I had a dim vision of her leaning on her elbow, watching me, as the too-real images of the dream and my waking mingled. I pushed her flat, covered her with my body and my hands frantically worked a handgun that wasn't there. By the time I was fully awake and knew where I was, she had struggled free and was holding both my wrists, her body astride my writhing frame.

"Steady, Halloran. You're here, with me. Steady."

I was breathing hard. She stroked my forehead and kept me firmly back down on the bed. My arms wrapped around her and held on to her as if she were the only living thing in a half-lit, dying world.

"You're safe," she whispered. "No-one can hurt you here. You're safe."

I relaxed slowly. My breathing returned to normal. I kept touching her body to reassure myself I was still alive. My stomach was knotted up and my muscles tense. Crazy, Halloran. You're cracking up. The strain of this operation is getting to you.

I turned over and Lucinda massaged my back and my neck muscles. The tension ebbed. Her hands were soothing and her voice reassuring yet sensual. I began to relax and closed my eyes again. Within minutes we were making love and I was floating on a gentle sea. Her eyes were deep and mysterious yet faraway. Then her eyelids closed and she sighed deeply, relaxed and satisfied.

Eventually she got up, threw on her dressing gown and went to try to cook breakfast. As we lingered over the coffee I said:

"I'm going after Ives. I'll let you know when I have him."

"I want to be the first to know," she whispered. "Because it will mean you're safe. Then we can have a holiday. Sun, sand and surf. How does that sound?"

"Add some sex and you're on."

She laughed out loud.

"Why do you think we are going?"

"Something to look forward to," I smiled.

"You will be careful, won't you?"

"If you're waiting, very."

I met Ames in the safe house in Oxford just after lunch. He had changed his pinstripe suit for green cord trousers and a green shooting jacket. The grey eyes were cold and thoughtful and the hardened hands were loading a Heckler & Koch VP 70 automatic pistol. He was looking five years younger, cool and very mean.

"Why did you tell Mowlam you wanted me as back-up?" he asked.

"Because you're the only bastard I can trust. And I know you can handle your end of things. I've often wondered if you were better than me in the field."

Ames smiled.

"One thing's for sure, H. I'd hate to have to live on the difference. Do you want to make the call now?"

"Why not? Everything is set your end?"

"Sure," he replied.

We had the house phone rigged to record the call. I dialled the

U.S. Naval Facility at Whitesands Head and told them to put Ives on. They gave me the runaround for a while about never having heard of him. I told them I would call back in one minute and that he had better be there. The second time I called a voice said only:
"Yes."
"This is Halloran. Is that Ives?"
The voice sounded like it meant business. Nothing loud or aggressive but just cold and not quite covertly hostile.
"We should meet, Ives. I want a deal. I'm tired of running around with people shooting at me. I got Kelly for killing Jack Lane and now I want out. But you've made it hard for me."
"Sorry to hear that," he replied.
"The deal is this. I need travelling money. I want twenty grand which is the price of a ticket to Rio and enough to get me started somewhere there isn't a lunatic behind every wall with a gun pointed in my direction. Unless you come across, every newspaper in London and abroad will carry the story of what you've been doing. I'll also tell my people. Not that they deserve it for ratting on me but because it'll hurt you. And if I die within the next twenty years my representative is instructed to publish and be damned as they say."
"I'll call you."
"I'll call you, Ives. Get the cash together by nineteen hundred hours tonight. Then I'll tell you where."
I didn't give him the chance to argue. I hung up on him.
The trick to misinforming an opponent is to do it in character. Ives would have checked me out through N.S.A. which would automatically have involved consulting C.I.A. London Station and the F.B.I. office at the London Embassy. This would, in turn, involve enquiries to informers in British Intelligence and Security. Not all the moles tunnelled exclusively for the K.G.B. In this business you turned anyone you could, friend or foe. And men like Bo Pepper knew me well enough to realize that an unrealistic cash demand from me would be ridiculous. But twenty grand to top up my pension fund was a very reasonable request. Ives would buy that story. Not that I expected him to pay me. No, he would make arrangements to take me alive and give me the truth serum

treatment to find out where I had concealed the informational goodies. After getting his hands on them, he would kill me.

We arrived at Frank's pub in Brecon at seven. A gaunt-faced, middle-aged man in a dark suit was waiting in the lounge bar. He stood up as Ames and I walked in and extended a long arm to shake my hand. My shrewd-minded lawyer friend Peter had read his instructions.

"Ames will go with you. You collect the girl Susan from the Llanmartin base and take her and her daughter to the pre-arranged destination. Once you're clear of the area you won't need looking after so drop Ames off back here."

Peter did not understand everything that was going on. I gave him a note for Susan. He nodded and walked out to his car. Ames looked at me and asked:

"Why are you doing this, H?"

"Old Jack always told me to protect the sources of information. In case I don't make it, I want the girl safely out of the Gwyns' way."

I didn't elaborate. I wasn't going to let on that I had fixed Susan a job with an old friend who ran a hotel outside Guildford because it was none of his business. Only Peter knew that part of it. And I could trust him to tell no-one.

I made the call to Ives very late, like five am the following morning and I told him to bring the money to the place on the Black Mountains where they had loaded Jack Lane's body into the ambulance after finding it on that frozen Saturday morning. That gave him exactly three hours to make the meet. Long enough for him to get there but not long enough to bring much outside help. I figured he would have to involve Daniels and the local police. Which was why I had brought Ames along.

I woke him at 5.15 am. Frank had only just gone to bed and we were the only three sleeping in the pub. Frank's wife was on one of her frequent continental holidays — the Canaries at this time of year was more suited to her mercurial temperament than damp Wales. Frank was hoping she would stay there this time.

Ames went over the map again and I pointed out the likely approaches to the parking area. Before leaving I checked over the

GP35 automatic Jack had carried. It was loaded and ready for use. I was carrying it as an extra talisman and also for Jack's ghost to have his share of the action. Just like he had done when we worked together all those years ago.

I drove the dark deserted streets a couple of times for luck before heading out into the country. The mountains weren't exactly home territory to me. The only reason I had chosen it was that it seemed poetic, in character with why I was after Ives. I didn't intend moving from the car park. No way would I have been able to run fast enough from the vantage point I would need to have occupied to see how many Ives was bringing with him. That 9mm bullet hole in my leg could have got me killed. Which was why I had brought Ames. Besides, he was more at home on the mountains than a goat would be. And Ames being ex-S.A.S. could make himself far more inconspicuous.

There was also another reason for bringing Ames. He had to arrange the escape route.

The Volvo's tyres crunched comfortably on the gravelled area as I rounded the edge of the car park area and drove right to the end, around the dogleg. I reversed so far in that nothing could get behind me. I left one set of keys in the ignition and gave the other set to Ames. Just as a precaution. He nodded he was ready, collected his Armalite AR18 from the back of the Volvo, unshipped his binoculars and flitted across the car park towards the slope like some demented ghost. I watched him for a while. Then we both tested our respective R.T. handsets and I switched on the Volvo's multi-channel transmitter receiver and tuned in to the local police wavelength.

The car window was open and my breath clouded in the cold morning air like puffs of gunsmoke. I looked up the hillside but I couldn't see Ames. I didn't really expect to. But I knew he was there, somewhere, ready to cover me.

My watch showed 7.50 am. The time passed agonizingly slowly, as it always did when you were waiting. I got out of the car and walked around in a small circle for a while. I could feel the wild, unfriendly spirits of the place watching me. I could feel Jack's ghost as well. No, foolishness, Halloran. Go and listen to that radio.

I had studied the map of the area for most of the night. I needed to because if Ives was going to involve Daniels then the old fox would have patrol cars on the two approach roads. Suddenly, the monotonous pip that came over the channel every few seconds was interrupted by a deep, crackling voice I recognized.

Ives, you cunning bastard, you have involved him. Daniels had two cars besides his own. One to cover each approach road but not close — a mile or two back from where I now sat. I called Ames up on the pocket R.T. and advised him.

"Halloran, sometimes I'll swear you're psychic."

"Ives is playing the only team left to him."

"We have company," Ames announced. "One cruise car. Uniformed driver and one civilian up front. Give it another few seconds. I hope to confirm identification of Ives."

I swallowed hard and sweated on that confirmation. He had to come. He couldn't just leave it to Daniels. Come on Ames, confirm identification of Ives. Don't tell me the bastard has suckered me again. My hands were clenched around the steering wheel. My foot tapped hard on the floor.

"Affirmative target," Ames announced. "Affirmative target."

It was the sweetest sound I had heard that year.

"Stand by," Ames continued. "Arrival in ten seconds."

I started the Volvo. Its throbbing engine turned over first time and ran perfectly. I gripped the steering wheel. Then the cruise car, white and shiny, appeared around the dogleg and I could see both men clearly in the front.

It stopped head on to me. Its driver was J. C. Daniels. His companion was William Ives. The photo had been a good likeness. Like two jousting knights ready to charge each other both vehicles now faced head on, sixty yards apart, engines running. A metallic whistle cut through the chilled air. Daniels' voice came over the loudhailer that was fitted to the cruise car's roof.

"I am a police officer," he announced. "You are under arrest. Get out of your car and walk slowly towards this vehicle and keep your hands held high."

My response was to pick up the microphone of a similar

instrument concealed in the bodywork of the Volvo.

"William, you've been a naughty boy," I admonished.

"I repeat. You are under arrest," Daniels replied. "You will never get off this mountain. The area is surrounded."

I made no verbal reply. There had been enough talking. Daniels' cruise car was big, shiny and powerful. But it did not have the big steel reinforcing bar the Volvo had above the front bumper. It was normally used for breaking down recalcitrant warehouse doors. I locked the seat harness and made my move. Before Daniels realized what I was doing, I had done it.

The Volvo was in second gear. My right foot hard down on the accelerator, I disengaged the clutch, fast. The Volvo charged forward. The power surge thrust me backwards into the seat. The sixty-yard gap closed crazily as I braced myself for the impact. I hit at full acceleration. The force of the collision shook every bone in my body and rattled around in my head.

The noise was deafening. The cruise car was thrown back yards. Its windscreen was shattered and its rear end crumpled against the shale of the escarped slope. Wrenching the gearstick into the neutral position with my left hand, I crash-tapped myself free of the harness. Browning in hand I ran to the wrecked cruise car. Its radiator hissed steam. Its bodywork was crumpled up and twisted like a grotesque modern sculpture. Inside, Ives and Daniels were in a bad way.

The impact had whiplashed both of them. Neither had worn seat-belts. Daniels, as a policeman, should have known better. But I guessed he had become so selective in the laws he had observed lately that this one just slipped his mind. His face was mixed up with bits of windscreen. The only recognizable feature was his grey hair and most of that was covered in blood. A gurgling, moaning sound came from deep within him. His heavy boxer's hands were still gripping the steering wheel.

Ives was semi-conscious and not bleeding much. I pulled the door handle and the door came off in my hand. The smell of petrol and oil filled the air as I dragged him clear. Ames was alongside me now, cuffing Ives' hands behind his back and dragging him towards the Volvo. The sudden realization of his predicament gave Ives violent strength. So Ames hit him a carotid blow with the edge of a hardened left hand. Ames only ever needed to hit once. Ives was unconscious. Tape was slapped over his mouth. He was bundled into the back of the Volvo. Ames was in the front now, listening intently to the radio. No-one announced they were joining us.

Daniels was still in the cruise car, moaning. His legs must have been trapped. The petrol tank was still leaking so I took a pineapple surprise from my jacket pocket. An incendiary job this one, to mix with all the petrol. I pulled the pin and rolled the grenade under the cruise car. Ten-second fuse. No time to hang around. I jumped back into the Volvo and drove off, very smartly.

"Jack Lane sends his regards," I yelled.

By the time we hit the road, the grenade had gone off. The fireball went up, sucking all the air around the cruise car into the explosion. Shock waves rocked the Volvo. Bits of metal flew everywhere. Flames scorched the mountain grass and a pall of black smoke rose skywards.

Ames looked at me and asked:

"What did you do that for?"

"He was about to call for assistance."

"That's why you brought me, remember? To ensure your escape route."

"I'm sure you would have done it perfectly," I replied.

Chapter 22

AMES HAD A safe house in the adjacent police area lined up. It was a country cottage, probably belonging to someone on the top floor at S.I.S. who used it as a weekend place. The phone was working and as he dumped the comatose body of William Ives on the floor at my feet he said:

174

"I'll leave you now then. That's the plan, isn't it?"

"Thanks, Ames. I appreciate what you did."

His grey eyes looked into mine and he grinned.

"You are as good as I used to be. And you're a damned sight nastier. Watch out for yourself. Don't let the bastards grind you down."

"Give my love to the Hall of Mirrors."

He drove off in an Austin Metro he had arranged to be left there. I called Mowlam and then let Lucinda know. Well, she had asked me to.

I liberated some malt from the drinks cupboard and poured myself a large one. I sat down and took a good look at Bill Ives. He seemed harmless enough as he was, like a baby asleep. But we were all babies once, and look what we grew up to be.

I lit a cigarillo and leaned back on the sofa. Half an hour later, Ives came round. I levelled the Magnum at him as he struggled. He saw the gun muzzle and stopped. There was a serious look in his blue eyes. He was, after all, a professional down to his polished toecaps. The three-piece suit was Savile Row in dark-blue. The lean, long face was harder around the mouth than his photograph suggested. The bony hands were agile and capable. Not a big man, his slim build was deceptive. There was a lot of muscle under the tailored exterior and a sharp brain under his neatly-trimmed hair. Like many Americans at his level of the business, he gave the impression of being a corporate family man who lived in a neat house in some leafy suburb and owned a condominium home somewhere on the coast or in the mountains for weekends.

"So you're Halloran," he said quietly, blue eyes taking stock of his situation.

"Hello, Bill."

"You really didn't expect me to come across with the money, did you?"

"No. Against your devious nature."

"So what happens now?"

"You didn't come up with the plane fare so I had to make other arrangements."

He stared at me for a moment then:

175

"So why did you keep after me. Because of Lane?"

"Exactly."

"You're a crazy man. They said you were a crazy man. You risked the rest of your life for Lane."

"Why did you kill him, Bill?"

"Had to preserve my operation. Had to hang on to the cover. Nothing personal. If you'd been where I was you'd have done the same."

I thought about that for a while. Maybe he had a point.

"Say, Halloran. Can I get up and sit down? I'd like to talk a deal here."

"No tricks, Bill. Your survival is a matter of complete indifference to me."

I threw him the key to the cuffs. He released himself and sat a good fifteen feet away.

"Pour yourself a drink, Bill. Don't go looking for your accessories like the stiletto knife you had up your sleeve. We took all that off you."

"Where's the other guy?" he asked, pouring himself a large one.

"Hired help for the day. Gone home to his old mother."

"No mileage in asking you to give me a set of wheels and a half-hour start? It would be worth a lot of money to you. A hell of a lot more than twenty grand."

I grinned at him.

"Bill, you must really think I am some kind of innocent. I'm a threat to you and your people because I know all about your operation. Your playmates Stateside would hunt me down and wipe me out."

"And have you told your people?"

"Certainly not. But I expect they will want to ask you specifics about your entire career to date, especially the most recent phase."

He was resigned to the fact that he had lost. And probably that he would be interrogated. All his suggestions about a deal were half-hearted. We had each other's measure and both of us knew it. But Ives was a pro. And pros rarely quit. And even more rarely do they let on they might.

"I guess if I tried to jump you, you'd shoot me in the leg."

"You guess right, Bill. I'd hate you to lose a leg."

He lit a cigarette and inhaled deeply. The blue eyes settled on me. We talked generally and amiably for a while. He had gone private for money, and a secure middle-age with a good second career in the Donoghue business empire. Most people sell out for money. Some for sex, or love, depending how realistic or honest with themselves they are being. The days of the ideological double agent are mostly gone. Everyone is now too disillusioned with it all.

I could understand why he had gone private. As he said, he was forty-five. The money was good and he could look forward to a minimum salary of sixty thousand pounds per annum, index-linked, for life. Uncle Sam had not seemed too bothered about the situation in Ulster up to that point. For all he knew the government were tacitly in agreement with what Donoghue was doing. His own personal view was that it was like the American War of Independence. But as I told him there are many views of history.

Round about lunchtime he was on his fourth large whisky and we had both run out of things to smoke when Lucinda Bellamy arrived with three helpers. They were big men with heavy overcoats and accentless voices. I knew two of them by sight and had no wish for closer acquaintance. They bundled Ives into the back of a hard-top Land Rover while the third man sat behind the wheel of a Ford Granada.

Lucinda was wearing a corduroy trouser suit underneath her Burberry. Her long hair was piled under a tweed cap. Her eyes flashed as she said:

"Can we meet later on? Say eleven at your flat? I fancy a change of venue."

"Sure. But no earlier. I'm otherwise engaged elsewhere until then."

"So am I. Some Embassy function I have to attend."

She kissed me. The sensation was intentionally tantalizing. She was obviously looking forward to seeing me later on.

I watched both vehicles drive off. Then I headed the battered Volvo towards London, via an indirect route.

It was going-home time in the motor pool. The civilian clerk, a fussy, four-eyed young man who probably arranged amateur dramatics in his spare time, wanted me to fill in a damage report. I told him I had retired and if he didn't forget about it, someone would be filling out a damage report on him.

By eight pm I had eaten in a steak house and was ensconced in the corner of an actors' pub off Shaftesbury Avenue. I reached in my coat pocket and felt the butt of Jack Lane's Browning as I searched for another pack of cigarillos. When they re-buried Jack, if they had not already done so, his gun would be buried with him.

I felt like getting drunk. Not sociably light-headed but blind, rolling, talking-to-lamp-posts-drunk. I was getting that way because by ten pm I was drinking beer with whisky chasers or whisky with beer chasers, depending on how you viewed your alcohol.

But I found it hard to break the habits of a lifetime, watching the door every time it opened, overhearing snatches of conversation. Two pretty girls, still wearing traces of stage make-up, with wide, interesting eyes, talked disparagingly about some artistic director they were working with. One referred to him as Attila the Hun. Wrong girls. I worked with him. He was re-incarnated as Mowlam. The second girl, a freckled-face redhead asked me for a light. I obliged. After two more drinks I decided it was time to go or I would be making improper suggestions to both of them.

I told myself I had finished with the business now and this had been my farewell party. And I had finished straight, not bent for money like Ives, or even bent for love, like that beautiful actress Lucinda Bellamy. I would not be seeing her again. She was Mowlam's problem now. And I expected that when she had delivered Ives wherever it was that they put people like him, Mowlam would be ready to ask her a few pertinent questions.

I tried not to think about her. We wouldn't have worked out together anyway. She collected Hallorans the same way a lepidopterist collected moths. By attracting them to a brilliant and beautiful light.

The taxi left me a street away from my flat. Another habit I would soon be breaking — walking the last street home in case anyone was following me. Come to think of it I would soon move out of the flat. It was time to drift south and look for some sun and some wide open spaces, to leave the streets far behind.

There were no watchers outside the flat. Even so, I waited for a while. It was 10.45 pm. A fine, grey drizzle was glistening on the pavements. I walked down the steps to the front door. And this time I did not fall over Moshe Dayan.

Very strange. I had been away for days. I had told him to watch the place. That one-eyed feline pirate was always on the doorstep or very close by whenever I came back. Because he always knew when I was coming back. He was a cat, he was psychic.

A taut feeling gripped my stomach again. I told myself I was being paranoid. But if Moshe wasn't outside, he was inside. So who had let him in?

I drew the Browning and pulled back the slide to feed a round into the firing position. Then I pocketed the pistol and drew the forty-one Magnum. With my left hand I carefully inserted the key in the doorlock, turned the key, and gently eased the door open.

The hallway was in darkness. I stepped inside and noticed a light shining under the lounge doorway. Visitors. Then I tripped over a briefcase someone had left lying around.

"H, darling. Is that you?"

It was Lucinda's voice. Something had gone wrong. Had I got it wrong? What the hell was Mowlam playing at?

She was silhouetted in the open doorway now, wearing that psychedelic silk affair that split and plunged in all the right places. The same dress she had worn the night we first met. She looked good, dark hair cascading over her shoulders. Sounds of jazz emanated from the lounge.

"Edgy tonight," she whispered, seeing the Magnum in my hand. "Your whisky is ready and I have a surprise for you."

Suddenly, Moshe Dayan flashed past me, a strange miaowing noise coming from deep in his throat. He disappeared into the darkness outside.

"I've fed him," Lucinda whispered, handing me the whisky and taking the Magnum from me at the same time. She put her arms around me and kissed me. The sensation was terrific. It always is when you are half-drunk.

179

It's funny how sometimes you know you have made the wrong move just as you make it. It was the booze, of course, and her perfume, and there was also another scent, wrong for the occasion. The scent of power.

Too late. I had walked right into the lounge before noticing Bill Ives. He was seated in one corner, in an armchair. His mouth was taped, his hands were cuffed behind his back, and his blue eyes were trying desperately to warn me I was in trouble. But I had walked too far into the room. Lucinda had closed the door and stood with her back to it. The Magnum was pointing straight at me.

"Don't do anything foolish, my darling," she warned. Her brown eyes were determined, her petulant jawline was set firmly.

I had no intention of trying to jump her. She was too far away.

"Wouldn't dream of it, beautiful," I replied. "So you really are with the Americans, but not with Bill's lot."

"Very astute of you, H. Have you known for long?"

There didn't seem to be any point in holding out on her. Maybe she would confirm my explanation of the situation.

"I did wonder why you fell into bed with me so easily the first night. At first I thought you took your job with Verity very seriously."

"Well darling . . . you do have a certain . . . rough-edged charm."

The remark was gratuitously patronizing so I replied:

"Happy to have been of service."

"Don't be a poor loser. You enjoyed yourself."

"Touché. You know something, Lucinda? I should have worked you out before. Long before I went to Glyntywyn for the second time. Because Elizabeth Gwyn, Kelly and Ellis playing Bill Ives had left for Switzerland on the Friday afternoon. Before any of them should have known I was still alive. And they had gone to set a trap that Bill had arranged. So how could he have known? The C.I.A. might have told him, via Bo Pepper. Ames might have, Verity might have, Mowlam might have, or you might have. No way was it Ames. I doubted it could be Mowlam. I wasn't sure about Verity or about you. Hardly Bo Pepper. He could have killed me Friday morning.

"So, Lucinda, the clincher had to be when I left for Switzerland. Gunther phoned me at your flat. The phone conversation would have told anyone tapping the lines that I was landing at Berne and the flight information tallied. Gunther saw to that. I told you Zurich. And Ives had a man waiting to tail me at Zurich. C.I.A. delayed him. Which leaves me to ask the question. Whose side is your former and current lover, Harman S. Talbot, really on?"

She raised her eyebrows.

"Who told you about him?"

"Goldstein. You know Goldstein, I take it? The gossip-monger who knows who sleeps with whom."

"Filthy little Semite," she replied.

"Not really fair. And it doesn't suit your liberal, liberated image to be a racialist. Harman's not racialist, is he?"

She smiled. I did not smile back. I had to tell her.

"I almost thought you and I had something going."

She had that faraway look in her eyes. The look that was there the last time we had made love.

"You were superb, Halloran. The girls are going to miss you."

"Don't mock, Lucinda. It's not nice. Now which side are you really on and why? And did you set it all up?"

She took a pride in telling me, a curiously offensive pride. Maybe it was because she really did love Harman S. Talbot fiercely. I should have realized. Maybe that was the reason I was still single. Too damned insensitive to the feelings of women.

"I helped Harman. He had a top-level brief. A very top-level brief. To stop the weapons run to Ballymurtagh by stopping Bill here and at the same time to leave Donoghue thinking that the Agency had not been involved, to think that the government had not been involved. How to take Bill Ives out without alerting the Almighty Donoghue who would then take it out on the Administration in an election year. Harman had infiltrated the American side of it. There were only three key personnel involved in the entire business. Harman turned two. Bill Ives was a different story. In fact Harman had to play it so carefully that it was necessary to leak the story that you were alive after Bill planted that bomb in your car. Bill was checking up on your identity, you see, even though he thought he had killed you. He wanted to prevent repercussions."

"Bit pointless letting him know I was still alive and kicking at the same time as having the C.I.A. cover me. But I can see why he did it. A clever fellow, your Harman. Even to the extent of advertising I would get taken out if I didn't cease my involvement. That was to cover him for the later eventuality, when Donoghue would be told that it was my personal vendetta and the Agency would offer to take me out to appease Donoghue's wrath."

I was sobering up rapidly now. This mental exercise was good for me.

"The original idea to use the British as the means was Harman's. I suggested using Natasha Madsen. A certain Deputy Director in the C.I.A. was brought in on the operation. A delicate balance, trying to keep you one step ahead of Bill. We thought Simon Verity would send a good man in. It almost went wrong when Jack Lane was killed. But Simon was insistent on following up. I picked you, from the records. And I will say this for you, Halloran. Those who said you were the best are right. Unfortunately, you have to go."

The Star Chamber across the Atlantic had tried to run rings around Mowlam as well. By now I was very sober. Bill Ives' .38 Special Centennial Airweight was on the table near Lucinda's right hand. She was too far away to jump. I knew what was about to happen. Lucinda would shoot Ives with my gun, then shoot me with his. Perfect. Bloody perfect. I would be seen to have done what I had set out to do and I would have died in the process. Ives would also be dead so he wouldn't be able to tell Donoghue that the Americans had acceded to British requests to close down the arms run. Ballymurtagh would still remain an N.S.A. facility and doubtless the appropriate person would be President. And Halloran who had done it all for them would have gone out at the height of his career. There was one question I still wanted to ask. Die happy knowing the answers, Halloran.

"So how do you explain all this to Mowlam and Verity?"

182

"You forced me to accompany you to obtain Bill's release. Harman provided someone who looks very like you to come with me not an hour ago to fetch Bill. They were leaving him to stew until tomorrow. You forced us back here. There was a struggle and you shot each other. Mowlam won't mourn you. He'll think he has put one over on the Agency. Harman will know better."

She had calculated everything so precisely. There was no point in telling her I had told Mowlam about her. The Magnum was lined on my chest and I didn't want to upset her now. She had even cocked the bloody thing. It didn't exactly have a hair trigger but any sudden pressure and that bad dream of mine would come true. Christ, that Magnum's muzzle was bloody huge.

Lucinda's smile was hardened now. She would shoot Ives first and then take his gun off the table to use on me. That would give me my chance. But first, act resigned to getting shot. Be fatalistic about it, Halloran. You're a hard man. You've seen a lot of death.

"Last request, Lucinda."

"A blindfold?" she smiled.

"No. A last cigarillo. Old Jack Lane always used to say the only way to go was with a Scotch in one hand, a cigarette in the other, and a beautiful woman. . . . Sorry, the next bit is too rude."

"The bit you liked," she laughed. "Go ahead. There's a pack on the mantelpiece."

I moved over and Ives started struggling. He had to pick now to do it. Where had he been earlier? Dull bastard. His last move was his worst-timed. Lucinda fired the Magnum.

The explosion in that enclosed space was mind-shattering. The bullet went clean through Ives' horrified expression and the back of his dark-haired head disintegrated all over the chair and the wall behind it. No sooner had she taken the shot, than Lucinda was swinging the Magnum back in my direction, holding it in an extended, double-handed grip.

The beautiful bitch could shoot all right. But I was already taking my only chance. Even as she had shot Ives my hand gripped the butt of Jack Lane's Browning concealed in my right-hand coat pocket. The second blast was as deafening as the first. The ringing sensation in my ears was unreal. The smell of cordite mingled with perfume. It had all happened like a slow-motion dream.

The force of the 9mm Parabellum bullet lifted Lucinda backwards. It entered her body on a slightly upward-travelling path just below her perfect left breast. The Magnum fell to the floor as I moved forward, fast. The hole in my overcoat pocket was powder-burned around the edges. The Browning was now in my hand as I stood over her.

There was a look of disbelief on her lovely face. Not dead, but in the final stages of dying, she coughed blood and gripped my left arm. The deep brown eyes were moist, her skin was soft. I could feel her temperature rising as I moved a stray lock of hair away from her face.

"Should . . . have . . . shot you . . . first," she spluttered. "Bloody . . . Headhunter."

She could say no more. She shuddered once, still gripping my arm, and died.

I closed her eyelids. The Browning was heavy in my hand. A sick feeling welled up in my stomach. It wasn't the fear. I didn't exactly know what it was, but I needed the fresh air outside to stop me throwing up. It was years since I had thrown up at the sight of death. I picked up the Magnum and walked out.

Chapter 23

I WALKED THE streets for almost an hour, breathing in the night air. But I could not dispel the perfumed scent and the smell of cordite. Those had mingled to become the smell of death that now followed me around. Eventually, I found myself down by the river. The water lapped the edge of the moonlit wharf. The city sounds were strangely distant. I lit the last cigarillo, the one I should have smoked in the flat. The match flared in my cupped hands and I drew in the taste of tobacco deeply.

The whole business had a bitter edge to it. With a little co-operation between Mowlam and Harman S. Talbot the whole thing need never have happened. It had because it always would and it would most likely go on happening long after I had walked away from it and probably long after I had died. The one consolation was: I no longer had to be part of any of it.

I would not shed any tears for any of them, except maybe Natasha Madsen and I hadn't known her. I would shed no tears for Daniels. He was bent, had broken his part of the bargain with me and had betrayed his office. I would shed no tears for Ives, for the same reasons. No-one would miss the likes of Kelly and his hooligans. And I would now shed no tears for Jack Lane. He had died doing the kind of job he had once been good at and wanted to be good at again. And I really should shed no tears for Lucinda Bellamy because she need not have started it all in the first place by suggesting Natasha Madsen. Life really was some kind of bad joke when someone so beautiful was capable of so much cold, calculating evil.

Jack Lane's Browning was weighing my overcoat pocket down. I took the gun out and wiped it clean of my fingerprints. I was not going to admit to killing Lucinda. She wouldn't have admitted to killing me, after all. And the Browning was an untraceable gun belonging to a ghost who had lent it to me when I needed it most.

I threw it as far as I could, out into the river. It fell like a stone, splashing heavily into the murky water.

I flipped the glowing cigarillo in after it.

Then I walked back towards the flat. I would have to get someone to tidy up the place.

As I turned the corner near the flat, I could see Ames' car. The XJS was parked next to Sir Simon Verity's Rolls-Royce. Next to the Rolls was a private ambulance. Two medic types were closing the rear doors. There was no siren or flashing blue light as the ambulance drove away. Ames was standing at the top of the steps with Verity. Both men were muttering darkly to themselves. Ames had spotted me before I crossed the street.

"You had me worried," he admitted. "Lucinda Bellamy and Ives were found dead in your flat. I thought someone might have got you, too."

"Is my cat all right?" I asked.

Verity threw me a look of pure hatred and stalked off to his car.

"Maybe he was secretly in love with her," Ames suggested.

"Maybe we all were," I replied.

Ames said nothing for a while. He gave me a cigarette, and then by way of explanation he said:

"Mowlam's people lost the run of Lucinda yesterday. She sprung Ives. Mowlam wanted me to make sure you were still in one piece."

"Mowlam is very careless. Either that or bloody deaf when I tell him things."

"Only when he wants to be. Fancy a drink. It's only just gone four. The Alamo will be open. You look as if you could use one. Then you can tell me what happened."

"Nothing," I replied.

I received a summons to see Mowlam the next day. He was in Ames' office. Ames was out of town for some reason. As I walked in, Mowlam's sunken eyes lasered at me and he said:

"I wanted to say I'm sorry we lost the run of Lucinda Bellamy. She is . . . was a very clever young woman. But you know that."

I said nothing so Mowlam tried another tack.

"I hope you don't think I had anything to do with her trying to kill you."

"She didn't try," I replied.

"She was shot with a 9mm Parabellum bullet. The Browning GP35 fires a 9mm Parabellum unless I'm much mistaken. Didn't you say Jack Lane had one?"

"Yes."

"I wonder how I should explain to Harman S. Talbot. He was . . . friendly with Lucinda. But you knew that too."

Mowlam was doing it again, scaring me. He was cleverer than I was. And the bastard knew it. Now why was he trying to scare me this time? Because he could no longer pretend to Talbot that he hadn't known about the N.S.A. operation to nail Ives.

He said nothing for almost a minute. Instead he stared at me. I stared back. Then:

"One other thing, Mr Halloran. Ames is moving on to another posting. You have keenly-honed survival instincts and an intuitive mind. You can also think things out. What would you say if I offered you a very special job? Not in the field, but in the Hall of Mirrors, as you call it?"

"I'd tell you what you could do with your job."

As I walked out I was sure Mowlam smiled, but only to himself.

Mowlam and Harman S. Talbot must have agreed on a cover story and given the go-ahead for a final cover-up. Later that afternoon I was working out a way to nail Alan and Garth Gwyn. I rang Frank to tell him I hoped to be down his way soon for a short holiday. He told me that both Gwyns had been killed in a car accident the morning after Bill Ives and Lucinda Bellamy had died. No loose ends.

I was thankful that I had made Mowlam aware of the consequences of any accident I might suffer.

That evening I packed up my things from the flat and went out the back way. It was time to move on. An additional safety precaution if nothing else. I had loaded up the M.G.B. and had locked the flat door when a dark shape emerged from the shadows. It made a cat-like noise and sat looking at me with its one good eye.

"You found me when I moved in, Moshe. You can find the next tenant the same way. See you some day, maybe."

Moshe Dayan walked right up to me, stood by my feet and miaowed.

"Damn fool cat. I thanked you for saving my life. What do you want now?"

He leaped up and landed, front paws on either side of my neck, claws buried in my jacket, and started purring. Eventually I disentangled myself and put him down. I walked away. But he followed, came around in front of me, and repeated the tactic. I put him down again and opened the car door.

Moshe Dayan jumped in and sat on the passenger seat as if it was his car.

"Damn cat. Come on then. You can come too. But you've got to earn your keep. You have to watch my back."

Moshe Dayan looked suddenly alert and purred contentedly.